As the horses began moving, Alex clung to his pole and leaned in. "You heard what Erin said. We've got to get closer."

I found myself smiling at him. *"So?"*

He smiled back as his horse rose up. Before I knew it, Alex puckered his lips and reached over to kiss me. He missed.

I laughed, trying to kiss him too. *It's not really kissing,* I told myself. *It's more like a game.*

Alex leaned in again. This time we bumped noses.

As the carousel turned and the horses pumped up and down, we kept trying. Finally we managed to brush our lips together.

The kiss lasted only a second, but I still felt a little flutter in my stomach. All of a sudden it wasn't a game anymore.

The ride stopped, and as I got off my horse, I looked at him.

He was smiling. "We're on a mission, right?" he said. His arms went around my waist, and he gave me another kiss. A much longer one. A real one.

His arms felt so familiar, so warm and comfortable. Then I remembered—we were just friends. That's what I wanted, wasn't it? So why was I kissing him like this?

10

TURNING
seventeen

Reality Check

by Jaqueline Carrol

A PARACHUTE PRESS BOOK

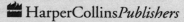
HarperCollins*Publishers*

This is a work of fiction. Names, characters, places, and incidents either are the product of the author's imagination or are used fictitiously. Any resemblance to actual events, locales, organizations, or persons, living or dead, is entirely coincidental and beyond the intent of either the author or the publisher.

Created and produced by
PARACHUTE PUBLISHING, L.L.C.
156 Fifth Avenue, Suite 302
New York, NY 10010

Published by
HarperCollins*Publishers*
1350 Avenue of the Americas
New York, NY 10019

First HarperCollins*Publishers* printing, July 2001

HarperCollins® and ▥®
are trademarks of HarperCollins*Publishers* Inc.

Library of Congress Catalog Card Number: 00-111223
ISBN 0-06-447344-9

Printed in the U.S.A.

10 9 8 7 6 5 4 3 2 1

Design by AFF Design
Cover photos by Anna Palma

Reality Check

Chapter 1

Kerri

I just stood there, terrified, my heart thumping hard in my chest as Donna Cantreal emerged from my boyfriend, Matt Fowler's hotel room and headed down the corridor. I tried to process the millions of jumbled thoughts running through my mind, but only one was clear. *She's really here in Chicago. . . . Really here in Chicago . . . Really here . . .*

Then I realized that if Donna glanced over her shoulder, she'd see me. I quickly ducked around the corner. The last thing I wanted was a face-to-face with the girl who'd been threatening and stalking me for months—all because she never got over Matt breaking up with her. All because she still wanted to get back together with him. And I was in the way.

Once I was out of sight, I took in a huge gulp of air and leaned against the wall, shaking. No wonder I'd been having nightmares about her ever since we first arrived here for the senior trip. No wonder I blew the modeling contest at Marshall Fields a few hours ago. It was my big chance to sign up with Diamond, a Chicago modeling agency. And that was gone too.

I cringed, remembering when I saw Donna staring at me from the audience while I was on the runway. How I freaked out, tripped in my platforms, and fell flat on my butt in front of everybody. Until now, I was afraid I imagined seeing Donna, because none of my friends saw her. I was sure that I'd lost my mind.

So now I knew I wasn't nuts. That was good news, I guessed, except for two things. One, Donna was actually here in Chicago. And two, she had just come out of my boyfriend's hotel room.

I definitely didn't imagine *that*. So what was she doing there? Did Matt actually invite her in? Just thinking about it made me want to scream. The whole *situation* made me want to scream.

I mean, I actually had a restraining order against the girl. But that obviously hadn't stopped her from stalking me all the way from Madison, Wisconsin, to Chicago, Illinois. Donna didn't go to South Central High like the rest of us on this trip. She didn't have any excuse to be here—except to harass me.

So what is she doing in Matt's room? I wondered again. He said he couldn't stand her, that he'd told her to get lost. And he knew she was dangerous. He knew she was out to get me. Why would he even let her in?

I was getting angrier and more confused by the second. I had to find out what was going on.

I peered around the corner. The hall was empty. Donna was out of sight now.

If only she was out of my life, I thought. *And Matt's.*

My knees still felt shaky as I hurried down the hall to Matt's room. His door was partly open, so I just barged right in.

Matt was walking toward the door. He stopped abruptly when he saw me. "Kerri!" He clutched his chest melodramatically. "Whoa, you really know how to sneak up on a guy."

I wasn't in the mood for joking. "I didn't sneak," I told him. "That's the kind of thing Donna does."

Matt's spectacular blue eyes widened. "Oh, God, you saw her?"

Oh, no. He wasn't denying it. My heart sank. "Yes, I saw her," I said, moving past him, farther into the room.

"Man, I was hoping you wouldn't." Matt shut the door and leaned against it, running his fingers through his wavy brown hair. He looked upset.

He wasn't denying it. And he was even admitting he wished I hadn't found out. My heart sank even more. "What's she doing in Chicago, Matt? And . . . what was she doing in your hotel room?"

I hated the way my voice sounded—suspicious and accusing. But I couldn't help it. I was scared and upset. After all, Matt had lied to me before about Donna. When she started bothering me, he said he'd only gone out with her once or twice. Then I found out he'd actually dated her for weeks.

"What's going on, Matt?" I asked.

"What do you mean? Donna's nuts, that's what's going on," he said. "Kerri . . . wait a second. You don't think . . . no." He shook his head. "No way. You don't really think I *wanted* to see her, do you?"

That was the problem. I didn't know *what* to think. Actually, I couldn't think. I could only feel— scared and angry and frustrated.

"Kerri," Matt said softly. He walked over, holding his hand out to me.

I didn't take it. I didn't want to hold hands. I wanted an explanation. "How did she even find you?" I asked. "She doesn't go to our school. How did she know about the senior trip and which hotel we're in and everything?"

"She probably heard about it from friends," he said. "South Central is a big school, Kerri. Donna knows other people who go there. And the trip wasn't exactly a secret."

Okay, he was right about that. But still . . .

"Kerri, please, listen." Matt shoved a pile of socks and T-shirts off his bed and sat down. "I didn't know Donna was in Chicago," he said. "I almost croaked when I opened the door and saw her in the hall."

"Why did you let her in?" I asked. I knew I still sounded suspicious, but I decided not to worry about how I sounded. I needed some answers.

"I didn't exactly *let* her in," he said. "She pushed her way in the second I opened the door. Then she was all over me. She tried to kiss me. She said she loved me. . . ." He gave a little shudder.

I stared at him. He still looked upset. And kind of sad too. What was that all about? "So what happened?" I asked, folding my arms across my chest.

"I shoved her away. I told her to get out or I'd call hotel security or the police. Or both. I told her she belonged in a psych ward." Matt rested his elbows on his knees and gazed at the floor. "It was like I slapped her. I guess I sounded pretty cruel."

"What's cruel about that?" I asked. I had major trouble feeling sorry for Donna. "She *should* be locked up. Somewhere."

"Yeah." He shrugged. "But it was weird, because then she said she *knew* she needed help."

"You're kidding," I said skeptically.

"I know—I didn't believe her at first, either," Matt replied. "But after a while, I did. I guess because she didn't argue or get mad," he added. "She talked very quietly, and she looked . . . I don't know, scared but kind of determined. Like she really meant what she was saying about getting help. Then she started crying and said she was sorry, for everything. It was really pathetic. I know you don't want to hear this, but I felt bad for her."

I started to feel a little bad myself. Not for Donna—I'm pretty sure that will never happen. But for Matt. I'd never even thought about how he might feel. I'd just decided that something devious was going on and he was part of it.

Not that I was about to go on a major guilt trip—after all, this was Donna we were talking about. Still, I realized I had to trust Matt more. Things wouldn't work between us if I didn't.

I finally sat down on the bed next to him. "Did she really admit she needs help?"

He nodded. "And she promised she'd get it,

Kerri. She promised she'd leave us alone. She's staying with her grandmother in the city, but she's leaving tomorrow. And I think she meant it. I think she's out of our lives for good."

God! What a relief that would be! I thought. I'd have my life back. My normal life, without Donna. Without phone calls or threats or restraining orders.

I took a deep, deep breath, way down to the bottom of my lungs. It felt great, like I'd been underwater and had finally broken to the surface.

Matt put his arm around me. I leaned my head against his shoulder, and we just sat there for a minute without saying anything.

This was what the senior trip was supposed to be about—Matt and me getting closer, spending time together.

"Kerri," Matt murmured into my hair. "I'm sorry about the way I acted when you couldn't go to the Duke Gaylord concert with me."

He said *couldn't*, not *wouldn't*, I noticed. A good sign. The modeling contest I'd entered took place at the same time as Duke Gaylord—Matt's favorite jazz musician—was playing. Matt had gotten lucky and scored some tickets. (According to him, this was luckier than winning the lottery.) He wanted me to go.

But he also *expected* me to go. To just skip the contest and miss such an important opportunity. We had a major fight. He went to hear Gaylord, and I went off to the contest.

So we lost that chance to be together. And that time it wasn't even Donna's fault.

"I had this big romantic plan about going to see the concert, then going out for a candlelight dinner," Matt went on. "When it didn't work out, I acted like a jerk. I'm sorry."

"It's okay," I told him. "Nothing really worked out the way it was supposed to. The modeling contest didn't either. Actually, it was a total disaster. Donna was in the audience."

"What?" He straightened up and stared at me.

I nodded. "And when I saw her, I just . . . lost it. It was horrible, Matt. I was walking down the runway in this gorgeous couture outfit, and cameras were flashing, and . . ."

I had to stop a second because I felt like I had a tennis ball in my throat. Swallowing hard, I managed to go on without blubbering, but my voice was shaky, and my eyes started filling up.

"And then I saw her staring at me," I said. "I tripped and fell. I was mortified."

"So . . . what happened?" Matt asked softly.

I swallowed hard again. "I looked like a total

klutz. And Jane Katz from the Diamond Agency said that I don't have what it takes to be a model."

"'Don't call us, we'll call you'?" Matt asked.

I nodded. I blinked my eyes, trying not to cry, but the tears ran out anyway.

Matt pulled me close. "I'm sorry, Kerri," he said.

I rubbed my wet cheek against his shirt. "And I thought you'd be happy. I told myself, 'Well, Matt won't have to worry about my modeling career getting in the way anymore. There is no modeling career.'"

"Hey." Matt pulled back and put his hands on my shoulders. "I'm definitely *not* happy about that. I know modeling is important to you. And I also know you're going to make it. Maybe not this time, but soon."

I wiped my cheeks and smiled. It was so great to hear him say that. To know he understood, that he was on my side. In spite of everything, I felt lucky.

"Thanks, Matt. I just wish Donna . . ." I stopped and shook my head. "Nope. I don't want to talk about her anymore. I don't even want to *think* about her."

"Fine with me," he said.

"She's history." It felt so good to say that. I put

my arms around Matt's neck. "And the trip's not over, right? We've got plenty of time to be together."

"Sure," he agreed. "But not just on the trip. We'll be together way after that."

He pulled me close again and kissed me. I felt so incredibly good. Donna gone, the fight over, Matt's apology—it was all past.

I stood up and took his hand. "Come on, let's go to Jess and Erin's room. I want to tell them what happened. They'll be really glad we made up."

"Yeah, maybe they'll throw a party." Matt laughed as we left his room and headed for the elevator.

I laughed too. Two of my best friends, Jessica Carvelli and Erin Yamada, were in major trouble with the high school chaperones. They had thrown a party in their room with lots of spilled soda, stumbling bodies, loud music—the works. Now they were on probation for the rest of the trip, which meant they couldn't go anywhere, or do anything without Ms. Gomes, one of the calculus teachers, breathing down their necks.

Almost no one was surprised that Erin would go along with the party. She was always ready to push the limits. Jess wasn't a goody-goody or anything, but she usually followed the rules. We'd been teasing her about it a lot lately. So she threw the party on a dare just to prove she could be impulsive.

The elevator arrived. As soon as we stepped in, Matt punched all the buttons.

"What did you do that for?" I asked.

"Well, we just kissed in my room, and now I figured we'd kiss in the elevator," he explained, putting his arms around me. "In fact, I want to kiss you on every single floor of the hotel."

It was so corny, I rolled my eyes. But I was smiling too. Even though the modeling contest was a disaster, Matt and I made up. And now that the whole Donna thing was over, we could relax and be together.

As far as I was concerned, Matt could kiss me from the penthouse to the lobby and back up again if he wanted.

The doors started to close. I wrapped my arms around his neck. "No more fighting, right?"

"You've got a deal—no, a promise," he declared.

Matt bent his head toward mine, and our lips met as the elevator doors closed.

Chapter 2

Jessica

"Okay, Jess, we got some CDs," I heard Erin say as she came into our hotel room. "What do you want—Bob Marley, Radiohead, Baha Men?"

I didn't answer. I didn't even look at her. I couldn't stop staring at the phone number I'd just written down.

Erin's boyfriend, Glen Daly, groaned. "Not the Baha Men."

"Why not?" Erin demanded. "It's your CD. You brought it to Chicago."

"I know, but I just realized I'm getting sick of it," Glen replied.

Erin and Glen kept bickering in a jokey way, but I tuned them out. I couldn't focus on anything except that phone number.

What did I think—that if I stared at it long enough, I'd figure everything out? Supposedly it was my nineteen-year-old sister, Lisa's number, but that made absolutely no sense.

"Jessica!" Erin called out, loudly enough to get my attention.

I finally dragged my eyes from the notepad and looked across the room at her.

Erin is Japanese-American, with brown eyes that always seem to sparkle and glossy black hair that she wears dozens of different ways. At the moment it was pulled up with an elastic band, spouting from the top of her head like a water fountain.

"Are you okay?" Erin asked me.

"Yeah, Jess, you've been standing like a statue ever since we came into the room," Glen agreed. He's a really nice guy, tall, with spiky red hair and freckles. "What's up?"

"Lisa dropped out of college," I announced. "She quit school. She's actually living here in Chicago."

"What? . . . No way. . . . Really?" Erin sputtered out.

"Are you sure?" Glen asked. "How did you learn that?"

I pointed to the telephone on the nightstand. "I just finished talking to Emily," I said. Emily was— underline *was*—Lisa's roommate at Marquette University in Milwaukee. "She let it slip because she figured Lisa already told me. And she gave me Lisa's phone number."

I still couldn't believe it. When I ran into Lisa yesterday outside Marshall Fields, it was a major surprise, since I never expected to see her in Chicago at all. She told me she and some friends were on a quick road trip.

The weird part was, she didn't look very happy to see me, and she rushed off as if she couldn't wait to get away.

That wasn't like my sister. I mean, we were never best friends, but we'd gotten much closer after she went away to school. Besides, we *had* grown up together, so I knew her. And I knew when she was hiding something.

Now I knew what it was.

"Oh, wow," I murmured, sinking onto the bed. "This is totally unbelievable."

Erin came over and plopped down next to me. "Did Emily say why Lisa dropped out?"

I shook my head. "Once she caught on that I was clueless about the whole thing, she stopped talking." I pointed to the notepad. "At least she gave me her number."

"And?" Erin asked.

"And nothing," I said. "I haven't called yet."

"Jessica, what are you waiting for?" Erin

reached across me and grabbed the phone. "Call," she ordered, shoving the receiver into my hand. "Maybe it's all just a big mistake."

I wish, I thought. But I knew it wasn't. Emily didn't sound confused, not about Lisa dropping out of school, anyway. The question was why did Lisa do it.

I took a deep breath and punched the numbers. The phone rang four times, then an answering machine kicked in. "Hello," a woman's voice—not Lisa's—said. "You've reached Fashion Statement, located at 1175 Smith Avenue. We feature top designer clothing, expert style advice, and free alterations. Store hours are ten A.M. to seven P.M., Monday through Saturday. We look forward to seeing you then."

I hung up.

"Well?" Erin asked expectantly.

"It was a store called Fashion Statement," I reported. "It's closed for the day."

"I don't get it," Glen said, dropping into a barrel-shaped chair by the window.

"You're not the only one," I told him. "Lisa obviously doesn't live in a boutique. What did she do, give Emily a wrong number?"

Erin frowned. "Why would she do that?"

"Why not?" I asked. "She's been lying for weeks

15

about still being in college. Why shouldn't she lie about a phone number?"

I jumped up from the bed. I was starting to get really worried. This was so not like my sister. Dropping out of school was strange enough. But keeping the whole thing a secret? Lisa just didn't do things like that.

At least, not the Lisa I knew.

"Has Lisa been unhappy at school?" Glen asked, swiveling back and forth in the chair.

"Who knows?" I replied. "I didn't *think* so. Besides, if she was, wouldn't she talk to Mom and Dad about it? Or at least to me?"

"Maybe not. Maybe she wants to figure things out for herself," Erin suggested.

"Be independent, you mean?" I asked. I rolled my eyes and paced back toward the window. Lately, I'd been teased about not being independent enough, which was why I took a dare and threw an after-curfew party in my hotel room. Now I was on probation—and so was Erin, since it was her room too—but I decided it was worth it. The party was fantastic.

But this was different. "Erin, we're not talking about a little secret like throwing a party," I argued. "We're talking about dropping out of college and not telling anyone. That's a major secret."

"Yeah, you're right," Erin agreed. "I'm sorry, Jessica."

"It's okay." I paced a little more, trying to think, trying to figure it out. Which was totally useless, since I hardly knew anything.

"When you saw Lisa yesterday . . ." Glen hesitated. "How did she look?"

I stared at him, confused. "What do you mean? She looked . . ." I tried to think. Lisa's hair was kind of messy, but that was because of the wind, wasn't it? She looked a little pale, maybe, but . . . "Glen, what's your point?" I asked.

"I just thought . . ." He hesitated again. "Well, what about drugs?"

Not Lisa, I thought. It wasn't possible.

Was it?

"I mean, you always hear about stuff like that," Glen went on. "You know—somebody goes off to college and then gets in with the wrong crowd and everything."

"It's horrible, but Glen's right, Jess," Erin said. Somebody's grades tank, and they drop out or get kicked out. Then they absolutely can't tell their family, so they just move someplace else."

"Lisa doesn't do drugs," I declared. Then I wondered—how could I be so sure? What did I really know about my sister anymore?

"It could be something else, though," Erin said. "What if she's pregnant?"

"Whoa, I didn't think of that," Glen said.

"It would explain why she's hiding out in Chicago," Erin said. "Has she been talking about one particular guy a lot lately?"

I shook my head helplessly. I could not remember. I couldn't believe we were even discussing it. Lisa didn't *look* pregnant, but that didn't mean anything. Plus she was pale. Weren't pregnant women supposed to look good?

Oh, God, I didn't know. I didn't have a clue what was going on! I crossed my arms, shivering a little. "This is getting kind of scary."

"Hey, I'm sorry," Glen quickly apologized. "I know you're worried."

"Me too," Erin said. "I guess we kind of got carried away. So . . . let's try to be sensible."

Any other time, I might have laughed. I was usually the sensible one, not Erin.

"Maybe you wrote down the wrong phone number," Erin suggested.

I shook my head. "I said it back to her after I wrote it down."

"Okay . . . so here's the first step," Erin announced. "Call the store in the morning and see if anyone there has ever heard of Lisa."

"Good idea," I agreed. "But the store doesn't open until ten, and our bus is out of here at nine." Tomorrow we were spending almost the whole day at Navy Pier. "I could try to call from a public phone, I guess."

It felt good to be thinking again. Trying to figure out how to get in touch with Lisa, rather than imagining all the horrible things that might be wrong.

"Hey, even better—we could go to the store," Erin said. "If they know anything about Lisa and they're lying, it'll be easier to tell if we're there in person."

"Yeah, but how are we going to do that?" I asked. "We're on probation for the party of the century, remember? Ms. Gomes said she's going to practically hold our hands for the rest of the trip."

"Oh. Right." Erin leaned back on her elbows, frowning. "There has to be something we can do."

I stared out the window. Beyond my reflection, I could see part of a street and the headlights of cars driving along it. That gave me an idea.

"Erin, could you call that number again and get the store's address?" I asked, hurrying over to the long chest of drawers. While Erin made the call, I excavated my map of Chicago from under a pile of clothes and spread it out on the bed.

"What are you looking for?" Glen asked, coming to peer over my shoulder.

"Look! Navy Pier—there it is," I announced, pointing to a red-shaded area jutting out into Lake Michigan.

Erin hung up the phone. "It's 1175 Smith Avenue."

"Right." I found Smith Avenue in the index. "D-3."

"D-3, D-3 . . ." Glen used his fingers to find the intersecting lines on the map. "There. It's not too far from the pier."

"That's great! Okay, here's the plan," I said. "We're going find a way to ditch Ms. Gomes for about half an hour tomorrow and make a little side trip to Fashion Statement."

Erin grinned. "Why, Jessica! That's against the rules!"

"Don't remind me." Erin was used to breaking rules, but I wasn't. If I got caught breaking probation, I'd probably be suspended. I didn't even want to think about what that would do to my college plans.

I wanted to be a writer, and for me, New York University was the place to go. My grades were great. I was even taking college courses already. But if I got suspended, it would go on my transcript. And NYU was so competitive. There

were probably a thousand kids *without* a suspension on their transcripts that NYU could take
instead of me.

But Lisa was the most important thing right
now. I'd worry about the other stuff later. I took a
deep breath. "I guess I'll have to take a chance."

"Fine with me," Erin declared. "There's just
one minor problem—exactly how are we going to
ditch Gomes?"

"I don't know yet," I admitted.

"How do you know Lisa will even be at the
store?" Glen asked.

"I don't," I told him. "If she is, then I'll try to
make her tell me what's going on. If it doesn't pan
out, then I'll have to call my parents. I mean, if she's
in some kind of trouble, they have to know."

"Okay, so let's figure out how we're going to get
rid of Ms. Gomes," Erin said. She put her chin in
her hands and scowled at the floor, thinking.

Glen returned to the barrel chair and stared at
the ceiling.

I flopped facedown on the second bed and
tried to come up with a way to escape Ms. Gomes's
eagle eye.

"Anybody have any brilliant ideas yet?" Erin
asked after a few minutes.

"Nothing that doesn't involve tying her up and

stashing her somewhere," Glen said.

"That'll fool her for sure." Erin laughed. "Don't worry, Jess, we have all night. We'll think of something."

"Thanks, guys." I slid off the bed and stood up. "Why don't I go on a candy run? Maybe some sugar will kick-start the part of our brains that comes up with devious plots."

I grabbed some dollar bills from my knapsack and took the elevator down a couple of floors. I got off, turned the corner, and saw Alex McKay feeding a bill into one of the vending machines.

I quickly ducked back around the corner and plastered myself against the wall. No, wait—what if Alex came this way?

Across from me was a partly open door. I could see shelves of towels and a big upright vacuum cleaner—a supply closet. I zipped inside, holding the door open a crack as I waited for him to leave.

Alex and I broke up a couple of months ago. It was hard, because we'd been going together since ninth grade. It hurt so much, and for a long time I wanted to get back together.

But I got over him.

And now I was hiding from him. I just wasn't ready to face him yet. What could I say? "Hi, Alex, it was great making out with you the other night?"

It was the night of my infamous party. Alex was there, and we got to talking. But the music was so loud, and everybody was so noisy, we decided to go to his room, where it was quiet.

Then we talked for a long time. And before I knew it we were kissing. And kissing. And kissing.

Then Alex's roommate came in, and I suddenly felt weird for being there. So I sneaked back to my room when Alex went to get us some sodas.

I don't know. I guess I was embarrassed. And no way was I going to face Alex until I was positive I wouldn't turn red and start stammering.

But I was more than just embarrassed. I was totally confused. I thought I was over him. I was almost positive. Then when we started kissing, it felt so good that I decided, hey, why not go with it?

So I went with it. And now, I wasn't sure how I felt about him anymore.

My nose started to tickle. I felt a sneeze coming. Great. All I needed was for my former boyfriend to find me hiding in a hotel closet— hiding from him.

Finally, Alex walked around the corner carrying two bags of Cheez Doodles and a Coke. The elevator arrived almost immediately and he was gone.

I sneezed loudly. Then I slipped out of the

closet and hurried over to the vending machines. I had to stop thinking about Alex. If I didn't come up with a plan to escape Ms. Gomes tomorrow, my only chance to find Lisa might slip away.

Chapter 3

Kerri

"**L**ook, Kerri." Sitting next to me on one of the buses the next morning, Maya Greer nudged me with her shoulder and pointed.

I glanced toward the front of the bus. Ms. Gomes had made Jessica and Erin sit right behind the driver as if they were little kids who'd been throwing spitballs. And she'd planted herself directly across the aisle from them.

"Look how she's watching them. I swear she knows they're going to make a break for it," Maya joked. Maya was the third in my group of best friends, along with Jessica and Erin. "She must be psychic."

"Yeah, I think teachers are born with a sixth sense about stuff like that," I agreed. Jess had told us at breakfast that she and Erin were working on a plan to sneak away so Jess could try to find her sister. But with Ms. Gomes sticking to them like

25

Velcro, it wasn't going to be easy.

I glanced around the bus. Luke Perez, Maya's boyfriend, was sitting farther back with Matt and Glen and some other guys.

Anne Myers and Amy Presser were sitting across the aisle from Maya and me. Anne was checking out her Chicago tourist book. "Hey, there's a temporary exhibit at the pier. It's an art deco carousel. They call it interactive art. We can ride on it. Cool."

"Don't forget the huge Ferris wheel," Amy added. "The gondolas hold six people, and you can see forever. At least, that's what my dad said. I was afraid to look down."

Maya laughed. "I love Ferris wheels, just as long as nobody rocks them."

As the buses began pulling away, I leaned my head back. "I am so not in the mood for this outing."

"Really?" Maya's big dark eyes showed her surprise. "Last night you were excited about it. You know, special together-with-Matt time? Besides, the place is supposed to be a lot of fun. Clowns, musicians, all different kinds of food."

"I know, it's probably great," I agreed. "But it's going to be so crowded and crazy. And there's enough craziness in my life right now."

"Like Donna, you mean?" Maya asked, pushing her brown hair behind her ears.

I nodded. I'd promised myself I'd stop thinking about her. But it was a hard promise to keep. Donna had a habit of barging her way into my mind.

"I still can't believe she came all the way to Chicago," Maya said.

"Believe it."

"How did she find out where Matt was, anyway?" Maya asked. "And what about the modeling contest? I mean, how could she possibly know you were going to be in it?"

I shrugged. "She's a stalker, remember? It's her job to know these things. Matt said it was simple for her to learn about the trip and which hotel we're in." I shuddered. "But you're right about the modeling contest—I don't know *how* she scoped that out. It really gives me the creeps."

"Sorry, Kerri," Maya said. "I didn't mean to bring it all up again."

"That's okay," I told her. "It's not like I've forgotten about it. I've been trying to, but it's not easy."

Forgetting about the modeling contest was just as hard as forgetting about Donna. Maybe even harder.

"I just hope Matt's right about Donna," I said. "That she's really going to leave us alone and get some help."

Maya frowned. "You said Matt was sure she would. You were so happy about everything last night. Did something happen?"

I shook my head. "I guess I just can't quite believe that Donna is finally out of my life."

"Believe it," Maya said with a grin. "Come on, Kerri, loosen up. Donna's gone. You and Matt don't have to worry about her anymore."

I knew she was right. I had to try harder to forget about Donna. She *was* gone. Why was I torturing myself?

I turned around in my seat to look at Matt. He was talking and laughing with the other guys. I couldn't hear what he was saying, but he was obviously in a good mood.

I caught his eye and gave him a wave. *Smile, Kerri,* I told myself. *Don't let him know you're still worried and upset.*

Matt pointed his finger at me and winked.

His buddies hooted and whistled. Matt rolled his eyes. "Bunch of juveniles!" I heard him say.

I turned around.

Maya grinned at me again. "*He's* obviously not worried about Donna anymore. Things can only get better between you now."

"I guess, but—"

"But what?"

"It's just that the modeling contest was so important to me, Maya," I said. "It was a huge chance for me, and now it's gone—poof—because of her."

I hated myself for complaining, but I couldn't seem to stop.

"Kerri . . ." Maya hesitated for a second. "You've got to stop thinking about this. It's going to drive you crazy. Try to forget about the modeling thing—at least for now," she said. "I mean, we're on the senior trip. You should be having fun."

Maya was right about having fun. I had to stop complaining and enjoy Chicago. Enjoy Matt. Enjoy life without Donna.

But modeling wasn't just some unimportant thing. Not to me. And no matter how right Maya was, I knew I could never forget about it.

Jessica

"How about this, Jess?" Erin whispered as our bus pulled up to the pier. "The tour map says lots of people in-line skate around here. Maybe there's a place where we can rent some Rollerblades. Then we could just take off and leave Ms. Gomes in the dust."

"Yeah, but what if we can't rent them?" I whispered back. "Besides, she probably wouldn't let us do it, because she'd have to skate too, to keep an eye on us."

Erin grinned. "Ms. Gomes on Rollerblades. Can you picture it?"

I glanced at the calculus teacher with her bold black glasses, crisp white shirt, and black pants. I had to laugh. Ms. Gomes was definitely not the type. She was way too serious.

The bus lurched to a stop, and I grabbed my backpack. Ms. Gomes immediately rose to her feet. "Jessica, Erin, I need to speak to the driver. You two wait outside until I get off," she instructed. "Then we'll tour the pier—together."

Oh, joy, I thought.

Erin and I still didn't know how we were going to sneak away. And if Ms. Gomes actually planned to stay with us the whole time, I was really and truly stuck.

If I couldn't get away and find Lisa, I wasn't sure what to do. I didn't want to call my parents. I hated the idea of ratting on my sister. But it felt wrong to keep something like this from Mom and Dad.

That's why I had to find Lisa today. I had to get some kind of explanation. I had to know that she was okay, and that what Glen and Erin said about drugs and whatever was totally ridiculous. Maybe I could even get her to go home.

"There has to be some way to ditch Gomes," I murmured as Erin and I climbed off the bus. "But my mind keeps coming up blank."

"Don't give up yet," she urged. "We just got here—we still have time to think of a brilliant escape plan. There's Glen—let's see if he's thought of anything."

Glen climbed off our bus and immediately put his arms around Erin. Before she could say anything, he kissed her. Erin kissed him back, obviously forgetting about coming up with a plan for the moment.

I smiled. They were really happy with each other. It was great to see, but I realized I was staring.

I turned away and saw Alex getting off the second bus. I did a quick turn and spotted Kerri and Maya with Luke, Glen, and Erin. I started to walk toward them.

Too late.

"Jess, wait up!" Alex called out.

Here comes the Awkward Moment, I thought. I told myself to be cool. Still, as soon as Alex walked up to me, I experienced a total body blush.

"Hi," he said.

"Hi." I glanced down at my feet, then back up. And I noticed something—Alex's face was definitely rosy. He was embarrassed too.

"Listen . . ." we both said at the same time.

I laughed. "You first."

"Okay." Combing his fingers through his brown hair, Alex took a deep breath. "I just wanted to say that I know things got a little . . . weird the night of the party. Well, 'weird' is the wrong word, but—"

"I know what you mean," I told him. "What happened was pretty surprising. Not that anything actually *happened*," I quickly added. "I mean, we're just going to be friends, right?"

There. I said it. I'd thought about it all night and decided that I didn't want to get back together with Alex. And I was almost positive I meant it.

"We're definitely friends," he agreed. "But I hope you're not sorry about the other night, because I'm not. I really had a good time hanging out and talking."

I smiled. "So did I, Alex." And it was true. I *did* have a great time. *But that was then*, I reminded myself. *What about now?*

Well, my face was cooling off and the knot in my stomach wasn't as tight. I was starting to relax, thank goodness.

"Good," he replied. "So let's stick to being friends. It's not like we don't have anything in common."

"Tell me about it," I said. Alex and I were definitely alike in a lot of ways. Kind of serious. Big on studying. Always worrying about getting everything done. I guess that's one reason we'd gotten together. Actually, Alex was even more responsible than I was—he shoveled snow and took out the garbage before anybody even asked him to. And I knew for a fact that he'd never throw a party when it was against the rules.

"Anyway, it feels great to relax and not worry about grades or papers or anything, doesn't it?" Alex asked. "We're actually stress-free."

The knot in my stomach suddenly tightened again. I wasn't exactly stress-free, not with Lisa on my mind.

Alex was staring at me, I realized. "What?" I asked.

"Nothing. You just got a funny look on your face."

That was familiar. Alex always picked up on my expressions and wanted to know what I was thinking. But I didn't want to get into the Lisa thing with him, not now anyway.

I made myself smile and pointed to the bus.

Ms. Gomes had just climbed off and was standing by the door, talking to the driver.

"My chaperone," I murmured to Alex. "She's making Erin and me stay with her, can you believe it? I'm surprised she didn't put us on leashes."

"Mind if I walk around with you guys?" Alex asked as Erin and Glen came up to us.

"Sure. I mean, no, I don't mind," I told him. Now that we'd gotten over the Awkward Moment, I was starting to feel more comfortable with him.

"Oh, definitely, come with us," Erin told him. "But you have to be on your best behavior," she added in a schoolteacherish voice.

Alex grinned. "I think I can manage that."

"Hey, you guys, we're going to check out the Ferris wheel," Kerri called out. She was walking toward the entrance to the pier with Matt and Maya and Luke. "Want to come with us?"

"We have to wait," Erin called back. She pointed toward Ms. Gomes and rolled her eyes. "Maybe we'll catch up later."

The others waved and walked through the pier entrance and onto Dock Street.

Erin glanced at Alex, then back at me. "So what's the deal with you two?" she whispered.

"Gomes alert!" Glen said before I had a chance to answer.

I turned. Ms. Gomes had finished talking to the driver and was bustling toward us. She didn't look too thrilled to see Glen and Alex, but she didn't send them away. I guess she couldn't think of a good enough reason.

As we walked with Ms. Gomes on the huge pier that jutted out onto Lake Michigan, I racked my brain for an escape plan, but came up with nothing.

All around us, people were strolling, skating, and biking, eating hot dogs or ice cream, buying T-shirts or balloons. We stopped to watch a group of musicians playing jazz on a trumpet, a saxophone, and drums.

Farther along, a small chamber group played classical music. A clown on stilts strode through the crowd selling balloons, a juggler tossed glass balls in the air, and a group of acrobats did handsprings and back-flips up and down the pier.

I heard the music and smelled the food, but I was so stressed that I couldn't focus. My worry about Lisa pushed everything way into the background. I couldn't even carry on a decent conversation with Alex.

Erin and Glen weren't talking much either, but for a totally different reason—they were too busy cuddling and kissing. They strolled ahead of Ms. Gomes with their arms wrapped around each other.

Glen would brush his lips against Erin's hair, then she'd kiss him softly on the cheek and he'd kiss her ear. Then they'd smile at each other and start all over again.

I thought it was kind of cute. Then I noticed Ms. Gomes. Whenever Glen and Erin kissed, she'd look at them, then quickly glance away with a pink face.

She was obviously extremely embarrassed. Could it really be true? Was tough, serious Ms. Gomes . . . shy?

Then Erin and Glen did a full lip-lock on each other in front of the pretzel stand. Ms. Gomes's face went from pink to brick red.

That's when I got the idea.

I knew exactly how I'd get away to find my sister.

Chapter 4

When Erin and Glen came up for air, I dragged Erin ahead of the others for a few seconds. "Keep kissing Glen," I murmured.

She wiggled her eyebrows. "No problem."

"No, really, be as nauseatingly cute as possible," I insisted. "You're freaking out Ms. Gomes. A few more passionate kisses, and she might decide she can't stand being around you guys anymore. Which means you and I can split."

"Got it." Erin grinned. "Like I said, no problem."

Erin and Glen played their parts perfectly. When we rode the enormous Ferris wheel, they didn't bother to look at the view. They just cuddled and kissed.

Ms. Gomes gazed at the sky, checked her watch, and tapped her foot until the ride was over.

She didn't leave, though. So when we got off, I

decided to get in on the game. Maybe four of us being ultraromantic would drive her away.

As we walked on, I slipped my hand into Alex's and gave it a squeeze.

He glanced at me, a little surprised. "What's up? I thought you just wanted to be friends."

"I do," I told him. "Erin and I need to lose Ms. Gomes, and all the romantic stuff is turning her way off," I whispered. "So could we hold hands or walk with our arms around each other for a while?"

Alex squeezed my hand back. "No problem," he said, sounding exactly like Erin.

When we stopped to watch an artist who did charcoal sketches of the tourists, Glen and Erin continued their kissing routine. Alex and I didn't get into that, but we stood close together. He put his arm around my waist, and I leaned my head on his shoulder.

I flashed back to the first time we ever stood like this. An outdoor book fair in Madison. Maybe our second date. We were standing in front of a booth, waiting for the crowd to thin so we could browse through the books. Alex slipped his arm around my waist and, without even thinking about it, I leaned my head on his shoulder.

"Let's move on," Ms. Gomes barked out after a minute, snapping me back to the present.

Glen and Erin broke apart—slowly. Erin gave me a wink.

As I started to walk on, the artist ripped the sketch from her pad. "Here you go," she said, holding it out to me.

"What?"

She smiled. "Your boyfriend bought it for you."

I gazed at the sketch. It was of Alex and me, standing together with my head resting on his shoulder. It was just a quick line drawing, but it captured both of us perfectly.

I glanced at Alex. He smiled. "I thought you'd like a souvenir," he said.

"I would. I mean, I do." Of course, he wasn't my boyfriend anymore, but so what? It was a great sketch, and it was really sweet of him to buy it for me. I rolled it up and put it in my backpack. "Thanks, Alex."

I gave him a quick kiss on the cheek, and as we walked on, he slung an arm around my shoulders.

This was a fun place, and Alex was being great, but I couldn't get Lisa off my mind. Why did she drop out of school? Why didn't she talk to me about it? Maybe I could have helped.

I sneaked a peek at Ms. Gomes, who was bringing up the rear. Wouldn't she ever leave?

When we reached the art deco carousel, Ms.

Gomes was still with us. "I didn't think it would be so crowded," she grumbled.

"I don't mind waiting," Erin declared.

"Me either," Glen said. He kissed Erin on the cheek.

But I was starting to worry. "The mushy stuff isn't working," I whispered to Erin as we waited in line. "What should we do?"

Erin thought a second. Then she smiled. "Pump up the volume, I guess."

"I'll wait for you here," Ms. Gomes pointed to the ride's exit sign when it was our turn to get on.

Glen and Erin sat in a red carriage and immediately began making out. Alex and I climbed onto two side-by-side horses, and we held hands across the space between us.

As the horses began moving, Alex clung to his pole and leaned in. "You heard what Erin said. We've got to get closer."

I found myself smiling at him. *"So?"*

He smiled back as his horse rose up. Before I knew it, Alex puckered his lips and reached over to kiss me.

He missed.

I laughed, trying to kiss him too. *It's not really kissing*, I told myself. *It's more like a game.*

Alex leaned in again. This time we bumped noses.

As the carousel turned and the horses pumped up and down, we kept trying. Finally we managed to brush our lips together.

The kiss lasted only a second, but I still felt a little flutter in my stomach. All of a sudden it wasn't a game anymore.

The ride stopped, and as I got off my horse, I looked at him.

He was smiling. "We're on a mission, right?" he said. His arms went around my waist, and he gave me another kiss. A much longer one. A real one.

His arms felt so familiar, so warm and comfortable. I was actually starting to enjoy it. Then I remembered—we were just friends. That's what I wanted, wasn't it? So why was I kissing him like this?

Forget it, Jess, I told myself. *You have much more important things to worry about. Like Lisa.* As soon as I thought of my sister, I felt myself tense up.

"What's going on, Jess?" Alex murmured. "Something's bugging you."

I shrugged.

"Come on." He pulled back and looked at me. "I know you. You're worried about something."

I smiled. He really *did* know me, and it felt good. "It's my sister," I replied, quickly filling him in on the situation.

"I'm totally freaking," I admitted. "I have to find out what's going on with her, and this might be my only chance."

"Yeah, I understand," he said. "Listen, I'll do whatever you want, Jess. If I have to kiss you a million more times today, well . . . it's a major sacrifice, but I'll do it."

"Ha, ha." I kissed his cheek. "Thanks, Alex."

I started to take his hand, but he pulled me close and kissed me on the mouth.

"All right, everybody, that's enough!" Ms. Gomes called out. "The ride is over!"

Alex and I drew apart, and stepped off the carousel with Glen and Erin.

Ms. Gomes had one hand wrapped around a supersized drink, which she must have bought while we were on the carousel. Her other hand was on her hip, and she had a monster frown on her face. "I am thoroughly fed up with your behavior," she said through tight lips.

"What do you mean?" Erin asked innocently.

"Making out in public is very rude," Ms. Gomes declared. "Now either the tonsillectomies stop, or the boys leave."

So much for my brilliant plan, I thought. *Now what am I supposed to do?*

"Feel free to let me know which one it will be,

girls," Ms. Gomes ordered. Just then, a little boy came running toward the carousel and crashed into her.

A gallon of red fruit punch spilled from the boy's megasized cup onto the front of her shirt. Her white shirt.

"Ahhhh!" Ms. Gomes gasped.

"Sorry!" the little boy called over his shoulder as he ran on.

Ms. Gomes held the blouse away from her skin. "I'm soaked!"

I pulled off my backpack. "I think I've got some tissues," I said, biting my lip to keep from smiling.

"Thank you, Jessica, but tissues aren't going to do it for me." Ms. Gomes frowned down at her shirt. A huge, wet, pink stain covered the entire front. "This will take forever to dry. I'm going to have to change. We passed a sweatshirt stand a little way back, so I'll go buy something there. The four of you go on without me," she said. "I'll meet you by the funnel cake in thirty minutes. And I expect you to be there."

Ms. Gomes went off, still holding her wet shirt away from her skin. I stood there a second, sort of stunned. We were free!

"Come on, Jess," Erin said, nudging me in the arm. "This is it."

"I know, can you believe it?" I asked excitedly.

I shouldered my backpack. "But wait . . . do you think we can get back in a half hour?"

"Don't worry," Alex said. "If Gomes gets there before you do, Glen and I will stall her."

"Right," Glen agreed. "We'll tell her you're in the bathroom or something."

"Okay, thanks." I took a deep breath, knowing I was about to take a huge chance. About to risk getting suspended and going to the college of my dreams, one of the most important things in my life.

But I had to find out what was happening with my sister.

"Come on," Erin said again, tugging on my arm. "Ms. Gomes is probably using a stopwatch."

"Right. See you guys later!" Taking another deep breath, I ran with Erin toward the exit.

Chapter 5

Jessica

"**R**un, Erin! Run!" I cried as soon as we were off the pier. I pulled the Chicago map from my backpack as we sped down the street.

"How . . . much . . . farther?" Erin puffed behind me. She wasn't the most athletic of my friends, but I knew she was trying.

"Eight blocks!" I glanced back and saw her roll her eyes as she moaned.

It felt like hours, but we finally got to Smith Avenue.

"I'm dead," Erin gasped as we slowed to a walk, looking for the store. "And I know what you're going to say—it's because I never exercise."

"Uh-huh," I agreed, jamming the map back into my backpack. But I was kind of wiped out myself.

"Look, there's the sign!" Erin cried.

Fashion Statement was halfway down the

block, between a travel agency and a Radio Shack. I cupped my hands against the display window, peering past the mannequins wearing shiny white polyester pants and yellow blouses with wide black belts clasped around their waists.

"Ug-a-lee," Erin commented. "No wonder there aren't any customers in there."

But I wasn't paying much attention to the clothes anymore.

I'd just spotted Lisa standing behind a glass-topped counter, breaking open a roll of coins and pouring it into the cash register. Remembering Glen's question about how she looked, I watched her for a few seconds.

She didn't look that great. Her dark hair was loose and tangled, and I couldn't blame it on the wind this time. Even through the window I could see that her face was pale. More pale than the last time I saw her.

I don't know why it was such a shock to see her there. After all, Emily gave me this phone number. Still, I didn't really expect to find her.

And I *never* expected to see her working there.

"It's weird that she's actually got a job," Erin murmured. "I mean, how long has she been in Chicago?"

"That's what *I* want to know." I headed for the

door, with Erin right behind me. I was relieved that I'd found Lisa, but I was totally confused.

What was going on? How many lies had Lisa told me?

A little bell jangled as I shoved the door open, and my sister glanced up from the cash register.

"Hi, Lisa," I said.

Lisa's brown eyes widened, and she made a funny little squeak of surprise. "Jess? What are you—"

"No way," I told her. "That's my question. What are you doing here?"

Lisa threw a quick glance at the door behind the counter. "How did you find me?" she asked. "Was it Emily? She promised she wouldn't tell anyone!"

"Don't blame Emily," I said. "She told me by accident—probably because she didn't realize you were keeping it a secret from your own family!"

Lisa's cheeks grew rosy. "I was going to tell you, I just wasn't ready. I'm still not."

"Tell me *what?*" I demanded. I didn't mean to sound so angry, but I couldn't help it. I was worried and upset. "You said you were here on a road trip. Why are you working in a store? What's going on, Lisa? Are you okay?"

"I'm fine, really, Jess," she assured me.

But she didn't seem fine. Up close, she looked

even worse. Her hair was dry, and the ends were split. She had dark circles under her eyes. She looked like she'd lost weight too.

Could she really be taking drugs? I was afraid to come right out and ask. "Are you sure you're all right?"

She nodded. "Things are just . . . complicated."

That wasn't what I wanted to hear. "That's okay, I can understand complicated things," I said. "I'm smart, remember? Honor roll, straight As, a special half-day college program?"

"Don't get sarcastic, Jessica."

I rolled my eyes. She sounded just like Mom, correcting my tone. "Don't avoid the issue," I snapped.

Erin cleared her throat. She was standing behind me, next to a rack of red-white-and-blue shirt-dresses. "Stick to the point," she murmured.

Erin was right. Arguing wouldn't get me any answers. "I'm sorry, Lisa," I said. "I didn't come here to fight. I'm just really worried."

Before Lisa could say anything, a woman came through the door behind the counter. She had a narrow face, a wide red mouth, and a stormy look in her eyes. "Oh, so you're finally here," she said. "Now I can tell you. I'm sorry, Lisa, but this isn't working."

She didn't sound sorry to me. Who was she, anyway?

Lisa's face turned red again. "I know I got here late, Ms. Hamlin."

Obviously this was the boss. And she was definitely not happy with Lisa.

"Yes. Late for the third time this week," Ms. Hamlin interrupted. "I was in the office. I heard you come in—half an hour after you were supposed to be here. And now you're even upsetting the customers?"

"But I'm not. I—"

"She didn't do anything," I piped in.

Ms. Hamlin raised her hand, not even looking at me. "I'll pay you for today, but that's it. I'd like you to gather your things and leave now. I'll mail you your check."

"What? You're firing me?"

Ms. Hamlin nodded. "Like I said, it isn't working out. I need someone more reliable. I called Gina, and she'll be here in ten minutes." She turned and swept back through the door.

"I don't *believe* this!" Lisa cried, angrily slamming the cash drawer shut. She reached under the counter and pulled out a big shoulder bag. "Just because I've been late a couple of times. It's not like people are breaking down the doors to get in and buy this nasty stuff!"

Lisa slung the bag over her shoulder and sped out from behind the counter. "I am definitely out of here!"

Erin and I hurried after her as she stormed through the front door. "Lisa, slow down!" I called. "We have to talk."

"Can't you see this isn't a good time?" she said as she hurried down the sidewalk.

"Lisa! You can't just disappear without telling me what's happening," I argued. "What are you doing here? What's wrong?"

"I keep telling you, *nothing* is wrong!" Lisa cried.

But she was lying, I knew she was. She always took care of herself, but now she looked awful. She was never unreliable, and now she'd been fired for being late all the time. She was my sister . . . and now she was running away from me.

"What am I supposed to do?" I shouted. "What am I supposed to say to Mom and Dad?"

Lisa stopped suddenly. "Mom and Dad don't know a thing. Don't tell them, Jess, please!" she begged.

"But . . ." God, what was going on with her?

"Look, I'll call you when I'm ready to talk," Lisa declared, brushing a strand of hair from her eyes. "I promise I will. I'll explain everything. But, please, please, don't say a word to Mom and Dad!"

Before I could argue, Lisa turned and ran away from me down the sidewalk.

"Lisa, wait!" I yelled.

But she didn't even turn around.

"Whoa, this just gets weirder and weirder," Erin said.

"This is *so* not like Lisa, it isn't even funny," I replied. "First she quits school and runs off to Chicago. Now she's been fired. I mean, she had the same job at the Gap all through high school. She's even more responsible than I am."

Erin bent over to pick up something from the sidewalk. "What are you going to do, Jess?"

"I don't have a clue," I said in frustration. "I know something's wrong. Am I just supposed to sit around and wait for her to call?"

"Maybe not." Erin held out the thing she'd picked up. "Look at this—it fell out of Lisa's bag when she ran off."

It was a business card. The name Bliss and an address were printed on one side. Someone had written Friday—6 P.M. on the other side.

Not just someone. Lisa. It was my sister's handwriting.

"Oh, my God!" Erin cried, pointing to the clock

in the travel agency window. "Jess, we're late. We have to get back to the pier, like, right this second!"

As Erin and I took off running, I tucked the card into my jeans pocket. I didn't know what it meant, but I didn't have time to think about it at the moment.

Totally sweaty and breathless, we raced through the streets back to Navy Pier. *Please let us make it*, I prayed. *Please!*

But as we rushed toward the funnel cake stand, I spotted Glen and Alex talking and gesturing to Ms. Gomes. She shook her head, then turned and started for the nearby ladies' room. Glen dashed in front of her and tried to say something, but Ms. Gomes sidestepped him and kept stalking toward the bathroom.

"She must be going in there to find us!" Erin gasped.

I nodded breathlessly. We were definitely caught.

Chapter 6

Kerri

"**Y**ou must have been ready to die, Jess," I said.

"We were," Jessica agreed. "Totally."

It was about five thirty. Maya and I had decided to hang out in Jessica and Erin's room for the night and keep them company, since they were not supposed to leave the hotel.

Jessica and Maya and I were sitting cross-legged on the floor. Erin was lying on her stomach across her bed. While we waited for Maya to finish shuffling a deck of cards, Jessica and Erin were telling the story of their big escape.

"When I saw Ms. Gomes marching toward that bathroom, I just knew it was all over," Jess said. "I could practically hear her telling me I was suspended."

Sort of like my modeling career, I thought. I had to keep telling myself it was just *suspended*. That it

53

wasn't over before it even started.

"So what happened?" I asked. Anything to take my mind off modeling.

"Jessica was ready to throw herself at Ms. Gomes's feet and beg for mercy," Erin replied. "But then we came up with a better idea."

What?" Maya asked, beginning to deal the cards.

"We told her the line for the bathroom was about three miles long, and we couldn't wait, so we had to go find another one," Erin replied, picking up her first card. "We said we were really sorry for being late, but we'd run back as fast as we could."

"Right." Jess nodded. "That explained why we were so sweaty and out of breath."

"And she bought it?" Maya asked.

"I don't think so," Erin admitted. "I mean, it was kind of lame, since none of the bathrooms had lines."

"But we were desperate," Jess added. "Anyway, Ms. Gomes couldn't prove we were lying, so what could she say?"

"I think I saw smoke coming out of her ears, though," Erin added with a wicked grin.

Jess laughed. "Oh, yeah, she was definitely fuming."

"You guys were so lucky," Maya said. She

finished dealing the cards and picked up her hand. "It's too bad you couldn't have stayed at the pier, though. It was great. Could you believe that Ferris wheel, Kerri?"

"Incredible," I agreed. The Ferris wheel was great. The whole pier was fun—holding hands with Matt, eating ice cream and tacos and popcorn, listening to the music.

If only I could have stopped thinking about the modeling contest. I tried, but no matter what I did, I kept flashing on that hideous moment when I fell.

And then I'd start to feel awful.

Just like you're doing now, Kerri, I told myself. *So stop it. Stop feeling sorry for yourself. You're not the only one with problems.*

I gazed at Jess. "I wish you could have talked to Lisa more," I said. "You must be really frustrated."

Jess nodded. "I am. I hope she calls me soon. I hope she calls me, period."

"She will," I declared. I felt bad for Jess. She had enough on her mind—like being in major trouble for the first time in her life—without worrying about her sister. "She knows you care about her," I added.

"I hope you're right." Jess sighed and picked up her cards. When she looked at them, her face lit up.

Erin grinned. "Didn't you ever hear of a poker

face, Jessica?" she asked.

"I can't help it. This is a great hand," Jess said, rearranging her cards.

Since Jess couldn't bluff, we all folded. Maya swept the cards together and started shuffling again. Jess tore open some little bags of potato chips and peanuts. "It's really great of you two to hang out with us tonight," she said to Maya and me as she passed the food around.

"A major sacrifice," Erin agreed. "What are the guys doing, anyway?"

"Luke's going shopping for a souvenir for his dad," Maya replied.

"Glen found a secondhand bookstore to check out," Erin said. "He said he'd call me later."

"What about Matt, Kerri?" Jess asked me.

"He's going to call me later too," I said. "Right now, he and some friends are going to try to get into one of the comedy clubs."

"Oh, now I really feel bad," Jess said. "I mean, didn't you want to go? I thought you two were going to spend lots of time together."

"We are. We spent the whole day together. And we're going to hook up when he gets back," I said. "Anyway, I told him I wasn't really in the mood for a comedy club."

"You're still thinking about the modeling

contest, aren't you?" Maya asked.

I nodded, and checked out my next hand of cards. "I know I'm feeling sorry for myself," I admitted. "So I'm not going to talk about it."

I couldn't stop thinking about it, though. If only there was something I could do. If I could just tell Jane Katz what happened, maybe she'd understand.

Should I call her? I wondered.

Oh, sure. I could hear her now. *A stalker? You poor thing, come over right now, and we'll give you another chance.*

Right. No way was that going to happen. I had to forget about it.

It was over.

"Well, I don't blame you for not wanting to go to a comedy club," Jess said. "I mean, who in her right mind would rather be out with her boyfriend when she could be stuck in this tacky hotel room playing poker?"

I laughed, and tossed my cards at her. Jess tossed hers at me. Then Erin and Maya threw theirs into the air.

While we were raking up the cards, Amber Brawley and Kathleen Kapinsky came to the open door. "We heard you laughing," Amber said. "Is there another party?"

"Hardly," Jess told her. "We're playing cards, that's all."

"Too bad. The party was fun," Kathleen said.

"Not for me," Jess said. "At least, not afterward."

Amber smirked. "Well, Jess, it looked like you were having plenty of fun today—with Alex McKay."

What? I looked at Jess. She was red in the face, definitely. What was going on?

"Well, we're going to a movie," Kathleen told us. "See you guys later."

As soon as they were gone, I pounced. "Fun with Alex McKay?" I asked Jess.

"Ooh, yes!" Erin said. "You should have seen them. Holding hands. Walking with their arms around each other. *Kissing.*"

"I thought you wanted to be just friends," I said, incredulous. "Weren't you just avoiding the guy because you were embarrassed about kissing him? You said you didn't want to lead him on."

"Honestly," Jess said, still blushing. "It was part of the plan. I thought if Alex and I started kissing, Ms. Gomes would get uncomfortable and leave."

"So you and Alex were just acting, huh?" I asked.

Jess nodded, but I couldn't tell if she meant it. It wasn't too long ago that Jessica wanted Alex back. Of course, she said she was over him now, but maybe she was just fooling herself.

"No way." Erin laughed. "If that was acting, you guys deserve Oscars."

Jessica's face grew even pinker. "Well . . . it started out as acting."

"And?" I said. "Come on, Jess, are you and Alex getting back together? Tell us."

"No." Jess tucked her hair behind her ears. "I mean, I don't know."

"Well, whatever, it was kind of cool having Alex around again," Erin declared.

"I thought so too." Jess nodded slowly. "At first it felt really weird being with him, you know? But after a little while, it started feeling normal. So I decided to just go with it."

"Are you serious, Jess?" I asked. "Just like that, you're back together with him?"

"We're *not* back together," she repeated. "I don't know where we are. But so what? I've decided not to worry about kissing him, or what it means. I'm just going to do whatever feels right and see what happens."

I was amazed. Really. Jess usually analyzed everything to death, trying to figure out what it meant and what might happen. But here she was, deciding to go with whatever felt right. I thought it was great. It was more like Erin. More like me too.

But now I was the one hanging back—knowing what I wanted, but afraid to go for it because it might not work out.

Not anymore.

"Thanks, Jess." I dragged my backpack off the bed. "I'm going to take your advice."

"Huh? I didn't give you any advice," she said.

"Yes, you did." I pulled out my phone book and flipped through the pages. "You decided to go for what you want, right? Well, that's what I'm going to do too. And what I want is to be a model."

"So what are you going to do?" Erin asked.

"Call Jane Katz at the Diamond Agency," I replied. "It's not fair that one bad contest should ruin my whole career, and I'm not going to let it happen. I'm going to tell her the whole story about Donna so she'll know why I messed up. I just have to make her listen somehow."

"Go for it, Kerri," Erin urged.

"Definitely," Maya agreed. "But listen, Jane Katz is a professional. You don't want to sound like you're whining or anything."

Oh. Right. I should have thought of that. "Okay, I won't whine. But what should I say?" I asked. "How should I sound?"

"Calm, but concerned," Jessica advised me.

"Perfect!" Maya said. She thought a few seconds. "Okay. Say you realize you didn't make the best impression and . . ."

"You think it's important that she consider the weird circumstances," Erin continued.

"*Unusual* circumstances," Jessica said. "*Weird* sounds too high school."

"Right," I agreed. "The *unusual* circumstances . . ." This was great. I was starting to get really pumped about it.

"Because once she understands the situation, you're positive she'll want to see you again," Maya said. "And . . ."

"And she'll be glad she did!" I finished. "Great! It's perfect!"

"Yeah, and then you tell her about Donna stalking you," Erin said.

"But don't get into too many twisted details about that," Maya suggested. "And make sure Ms. Katz knows it's over. You don't want her to think it could happen again."

"Got it." I rummaged in my backpack for a pencil. "Let me write it down so I don't forget anything."

"Don't do that," Maya said. "If you read it, it'll

sound too stiff. Just jot down some key words. That's what Dad does with his speeches." Maya's father was running for lieutenant governor.

"Maya's right," Jess agreed. "Go over it with us a couple of times, then make the call."

As we went over my speech, I felt like an actor getting ready for a big role. This wasn't a play, though. It was my life.

When I finally picked up the phone to call the Diamond Agency, my hands were shaking. The phone began to ring, and I took a deep breath.

A woman's voice answered. "Diamond Agency."

"Yes, may I please speak to Jane Katz?" I said.

"I'm sorry, Ms. Katz is gone for the day," the woman replied. "This is her assistant, Laura. Maybe I can help you."

I practically collapsed on the bed. I'd been so pumped about talking to Jane. Now I knew what a punctured balloon felt like.

"Hello?" Laura's voice came over the line.

I forced myself to sit up straight. "Thank you, but I need to talk to Ms. Katz," I said. I gave her my name, the telephone number of the hotel, and my room number. "Could you please ask her to call me tomorrow? It's very important."

"I'll give her the message," Laura said. She hung up before I did.

"Not there, huh?" Erin asked.

I shook my head. "I left a message. I just hope she gets it."

"I'm sure she will," Jess told me.

Right, I thought. *But will she answer it?*

Chapter 7

Jessica

"What's this play about, anyway?" Matt asked the next afternoon.

The whole class was at a matinee at the Steppenwolf theater, waiting for the first act to start. Alex and I sat next to Maya and Luke. Glen and Erin and Matt and Kerri sat in the row behind us. Ms. Gomes was eight rows back, thank goodness.

"I don't know what it's about exactly, but it's some kind of multimedia thing," Erin said, flipping through the program. "According to this, it's 'experimental' and 'heavily symbolic.'"

Glen wanted to be a filmmaker, so he perked up at the multimedia part. But Luke and Matt groaned.

"Symbolic—that means nobody'll get it," Alex joked.

"Yeah, but we have to pay attention," Matt

said. "With our luck, there'll be a paper due on it when we get back."

Luke groaned again. He's a really bright guy, but he's not exactly crazy about school. "They wouldn't do that to us. Would they?"

"Nah. They know we'd revolt," Alex told him. "Relax, Luke, this is a vacation."

Alex slipped his arm around my shoulders. He did it so casually, as if it was the most normal thing in the world.

Maybe it was. It sure felt normal, the way kissing and holding hands at the pier did. It was like nothing bad had ever happened between us. Like we'd never broken up at all.

I wasn't exactly sure how I felt about that. I mean, things have been so different between Alex and me. I never really stopped long enough to consider his new girlfriend. Her name was Suzanne, and her mother didn't let her come on the senior trip.

Wouldn't Suzanne be upset if she knew he had his arm around me? She would definitely be upset if she found out that we kissed. I know I would be.

When Matt turned around, draped himself over his seat back and started talking to Luke and Alex, Maya leaned close to me. "It would be so cool if you and Alex got back together, Jessica," she whispered.

"Then we'd all have boyfriends. We could all go to the prom together, the way we used to talk about. Can you picture it? We'd have a totally awesome time!"

The house lights dimmed before I could say anything. But as the curtain rose and some eerie sitar music began, I thought about what Maya said.

All of us going to the prom together? Kerri and Maya and Erin and I shopping for dresses, Alex and Glen and Matt and Luke picking us up in a superstretch limousine? A preprom party, a sunrise breakfast?

I guess it would be pretty cool to do that with my best friends. But the prom seemed so far away. Who knew what would happen in the meantime?

Besides, I couldn't really think about it—I was way too worried about Lisa.

She hadn't called. Not last night and not this morning. At first I didn't even want to come to the play, in case she picked this afternoon to contact me. But Erin talked me out of staying at the hotel. "You'll go nuts sitting around waiting," she argued. "Besides, Ms. Gomes won't let you stay in the hotel by yourself."

I knew Erin was right about Ms. Gomes, so I didn't even bother to ask. If Lisa did call the hotel, I'd just have to hope she'd keep trying. Or at least leave a number for me to call her back.

But what if she *didn't* call? Ever? What would I do then?

I was thinking so much about Lisa, I couldn't concentrate on the play at all. Too bad, because it looked spectacular. Actors in masks, a Greek-type chorus, lots of cool lighting effects. I'm sure it had a plot, but I didn't have a clue what it was.

When intermission came, most of us went to the lobby to buy something to drink. Alex walked next to me, his hand touching the small of my back. "Want to get a Coke?" he asked.

I had the funniest feeling all of a sudden. And then I realized it was the same feeling I'd had when we stood in front of the artist yesterday. *We've done this before,* I thought. *So many times. Gone to a play or a movie, walked up the aisle.*

It felt good. It would be so easy to get back into something like this.

"Jess?" Alex asked. "Want a Coke?"

I looked at all the kids bearing down on the concession stand and shook my head. "Too crowded. I'll just have some water." There was a water fountain at one end of the lobby. Alex and I both took a drink, then leaned against the wall together.

"Lucky for you there *isn't* a paper due on this

play," he said, nudging me gently with his shoulder.

"What do you mean?"

"I mean your mind was about a zillion miles away in there."

I had to smile. That had happened before too. When we used to study together, Alex could always tell when my mind was wandering—even when I tried to look like I was really into it.

"It's Lisa, right?" he asked. I'd told him about finding her and how she said she'd call.

"I'm so worried, Alex," I said. "I mean, she got fired from that store, so I can't go back there to talk to her. And what if she doesn't call? I wouldn't know where to find her! The only clue I've got is the card that fell out of her bag."

I pulled out the card for Bliss from my pocket and showed it to him. "The guy at the hotel desk said it's some kind of club. I don't know. But I'm thinking I should go there."

Alex raised his eyebrows. "Sneak out of the hotel, you mean?"

"Yes! Alex, this is my sister we're talking about!"

He put his arm around me. "Hey, I understand. I don't blame you for being worried about your sister. Don't forget, I know what it's like."

True. Alex's older brother, David, had given his

family plenty to worry about when he and his girlfriend got married and had a baby right out of high school. Actually, she got pregnant, then they got married. Now the three of them were living at Alex's house, and things were not exactly smooth all the time.

"Listen, Jess, I don't want to scare you, but the way Lisa's been acting kind of reminds me of my cousin, Philip," Alex said.

"What do you mean?"

"I told you about it, remember? Philip was away at college, like Lisa, and he all of a sudden went through this total personality change," Alex reminded me. "His grades went down the tubes, and he lost his job at the library. He stopped calling home. His roommate said he usually stayed out all night. And whenever his mom or dad managed to reach him, he was like, so what? He just didn't care about anything."

I remembered now. Philip was doing drugs. And I remembered something else—I saw him once, before he got straight. He was really thin, with pasty skin and dark smudges around his eyes. Really messed up.

Lisa didn't look as bad as Philip, but she didn't look good, either. Could she really be on drugs?

"Oh, God, Alex," I whispered. "Glen talked

about drugs too, and I told him it was impossible."

It is, I thought. *It has to be. Lisa can't be doing that stuff.*

But what if she was? She was lying, wasn't she? She'd dropped out of school, she'd been fired from her job because she was always late, and she looked sick.

And she didn't want to see me, her own sister.

"I guess . . ." I started to say. I put my hands over my face. I wanted to keep saying it was impossible, but I couldn't.

Lisa might have gotten in with the wrong crowd. She might be on drugs. It *was* possible. I had to face it. And I had to find her.

Alex put his arms around me. "Listen, I don't want to tell you what to do, but if Lisa's into something like that . . . I mean, this is serious. Don't you think you should call your parents? Besides," he added, "you're on probation. If you sneak out to this Bliss place and get caught—"

"I know," I murmured.

"Then why risk it?" Alex asked. "Why risk NYU? That's your dream, Jess."

Before I could say anything else, Kerri called out over the crowd. "Jess, Alex! Didn't you see the lights flashing? It's time to go back in!"

I raised my head. When Kerri saw my face, she

gave me a questioning look, like "Are you okay?"

I forced a smile and waved to her. There wasn't time to talk now.

Alex took my hand, and we slowly made our way back inside with the rest of the crowd. As the lights dimmed, he put his arm around me again.

I leaned my head on his shoulder and tried to relax. But I was still upset, and I knew I wasn't going to pay any attention to the second act of the play either.

Still, being with Alex helped. It was great knowing he was there for me. I didn't have to explain things to him, because he already knew me. He knew my family. I felt comfortable with him. I realized I'd really missed that. It was sort of how I felt when I put on my favorite jeans, the ones that I'd washed so many times they were soft as feathers.

I almost wished he *didn't* know me so well. Because he was right—I had to call my parents sooner or later. And there definitely wouldn't be anything comfortable about that.

Kerri

"Quick, Maya!" I cried. "I hear the phone ringing. It's got to be Jane! Unlock the door!"

We'd just come back from the play at Steppenwolf. We had gone back to our room to freshen up before we met Jess, Erin, and the guys for dinner. Maya was digging around in her bag for the key card.

"It's ringing!" I was practically hopping up and down. I couldn't miss this call. "Hurry, Maya!"

"Kerri! Stop breathing down my neck!" Maya finally fished the card out and stuck it into the lock. "There!"

Maya threw open the door and jumped aside as I raced into the room. I'd totally forgotten my speech, but I couldn't worry about that. The important thing was that Jane Katz was calling me back. I'd figure out what to say.

I grabbed the phone in the middle of a ring. "Hello?"

"Kerri. Don't hang up."

For a split second, I didn't recognize her voice. When I did, I felt like I'd been punched in the stomach.

It was Donna.

God, it was supposed to be over! She promised Matt she'd leave us alone!

"If you're smart, you'll listen to me, Kerri," Donna went on. "Matt's lying to you. He's been hiding something for a while now. And I think it's about time you found out his dirty little secret."

"Shut up!" I screamed. I wasn't scared of her, not at the moment. I was totally furious. "He's not hiding anything. You're just trying to ruin things between us. But you can forget it. Matt is the only thing you haven't ruined for me, and guess what? It's never going to happen!"

I slammed the phone down, and realized that my hands were shaking. My whole body was shaking. I hugged myself and gazed at Maya. "Matt was wrong about Donna," I told her. "It's not over."

Chapter 8

"Oh, Kerri, this is awful!" Maya said.

"I know. I just don't believe it," I said, pacing back and forth between the beds. "Wait—yes I do. Donna's a stalker, right? Stalkers don't give up. Why did I ever believe she'd leave us alone? Am I a total idiot?"

Maya shrugged out of her jacket. "Matt's going to freak."

Matt. I had to tell him. With a shaky hand, I picked up the phone again and dialed his room. "She fooled us both, Matt," I said the minute he answered.

"Kerri? What are you talking about?"

"Donna. She just called me," I told him.

He didn't say anything for a few seconds. I could practically see the shock on his face. "God, Kerri!" he finally said. "Are you okay?"

Hardly. I was so angry I felt like hitting

something. A punching bag with Donna's face on it would be good. "I'm just so furious," I said to Matt. "She lied to you. All that crying and saying she was sorry was a complete crock. She's not going to get help. She doesn't want help."

She wants you, I added silently.

"Man, this is incredible," Matt said. "I'm sorry, Kerri, I really thought she was going to get her act together. I can't believe she fooled me. I should never have believed her."

Probably not, I thought. But so what? Even if he'd kicked her out or called the police, she wouldn't be out of our lives, not for good. "It's not your fault," I told him. "She's the one who's a psycho."

"What did she say to you?" Matt asked. "Did she threaten you?"

"No." I sat down on the bed. "She said you were lying to me. That you'd been hiding something from me for a long time."

Matt was silent for a second. What was he thinking?

"Matt?" I asked. "Did you hear me?"

"I heard you," he said. His voice shook a little, and it was very soft. But I could tell he was ready to explode.

"I'm not hiding anything from you, Kerri,"

Matt declared quietly. "Whatever Donna told you is a lie. She's just trying to come between us again."

I knew it, I thought.

"That's exactly what I said to her," I told him. "Anyway, I didn't give her a chance to tell whatever lie she'd cooked up," I said. "I yelled at her and then I hung up on her."

"Good. Man, this is incredible," he said again. "Are you sure you're all right? You want me to come to your room before we go to dinner with everybody?"

"I'm okay, really. But we have to talk," I told him. "We need to figure out what to do."

"Right. I'll come over," he said. "I'll be there in a few minutes."

"Okay. Thanks, Matt." I hung up and looked at Maya. "He's coming here. We're going to talk about what to do. What do you think? Should I call the police?"

"You probably should." Maya punched up a pillow and sat back on her bed. "Could they arrest her? I mean, will the restraining order work out here in Chicago?"

"You're asking me?" I stood up and began pacing again.

"Well, I bet they'd give her a hard time at least," Maya said.

That would be nice, I thought. But could the police find Donna? Matt had said she was staying with her grandmother. I wondered if her grandmother had the same last name as she did. Otherwise it might be tough. But then again, who knew if Donna was even telling the truth?

"What about your mom?" Maya asked. "I guess you should call her."

I started to say yes. Then I changed my mind. *Not so fast, Kerri*. I told myself. *Think about it first.*

What would happen if I called my mother?

That was easy—she'd make me come home. As soon as possible. Sooner. Like right now. If FedEx had same-day delivery for humans, Mom would make me use it.

Which meant I wouldn't be able to talk to Jane Katz and try to convince her to give me another chance at modeling. My last chance.

Plus, if I called Mom, I'd have to explain everything. And that meant telling her how I'd faked her signature on the permission slip for the modeling contest.

My mom wasn't exactly crazy about modeling. She thought it was way too superficial. She let me do it a little at home, but sign up with an agency in Chicago? Forget it.

She didn't understand how much I wanted it.

77

How modeling would easily pay my way through college at the University of Miami. That's why I signed the permission slip myself.

"If I tell Mom about Donna and the modeling contest, she'll make me come home," I said to Maya. "Then she'll ground me. Forever."

"Come on. Your mom's never grounded you," she reminded me.

That was true. But my mom never said no to me before either—until I told her I wanted to model. "There's always a first time," I said.

"Well . . . so what are you going to do?" Maya asked.

"Nothing."

"Huh?" Maya frowned. "You have to do something, don't you?"

"Why?" I asked. "The police probably can't help. My mother would definitely make me come home. I wouldn't be able to talk to Jane Katz. And then my whole modeling thing would be completely ruined."

Maya started to say something, then gave her head a little shake.

"What?" I asked.

"Nothing. Never mind."

"No, what is it, Maya? I can tell you've got something on your mind."

Maya still hesitated. Finally she said, "I was just wondering . . . *what* modeling thing?"

I stared at her. What was she talking about? She knew exactly how important modeling was to me.

Maya sat up and wrapped her arms around her knees. "You didn't win the contest," she reminded me gently. "And Jane Katz hasn't called you back. There's no message light on the phone, right?"

I glanced at the buttons. No blinking light. No message from Jane Katz.

"So like I said . . . what modeling thing?" Maya repeated in a quiet voice.

I kept staring at the phone. I hated to admit it, but Maya was right. Jane Katz hadn't called. She probably never would. My so-called career was going down the tubes.

Still. It wasn't gone yet. And it was up to me to save it. There was still a chance. Okay, a very slim chance. But I had to take it.

I straightened up. "I know what you're saying, Maya," I said. "But if I give up, then Donna wins. Besides, maybe it sounds crazy, but I've got a feeling that this is going to happen for me here in Chicago. I have to give it one more try. I have to go after it. If I don't, I'll always wonder what might have been."

"That doesn't sound crazy," Maya told me. "I

guess I just don't see what else you can do."

I stood up and went to the dresser. "I'm going over to the Diamond Agency in person," I said as I reached for my hairbrush.

"Now? Really?"

"Really." I began brushing my hair.

"What about Donna?" Maya asked.

"If I can't convince them to give me a chance, then I'll tell my mom about Donna," I declared. "But right now, I'm not even going to think about the girl. Not until after I've talked to Jane Katz."

Jessica

If Lisa's into something like that . . . don't you think you should call your parents?

Alex's question was still on my mind when I walked into my hotel room after the play.

The answer was obviously yes. How could I keep something like drugs a secret? It wasn't like cutting classes or breaking curfew.

I had to tell. If I didn't, Lisa might get in deeper and deeper, until it was too late to bring her back.

So do it, Jess, I told myself. *Pick up the phone and call.*

Erin was with Glen, picking out souvenirs in the hotel gift shop. I tossed my coat on my bed, sat down next to the phone, and picked it up. Before I could talk myself out of it, I punched in my home number.

The card from Bliss lay on next to the phone on the nightstand. I picked it up and fiddled with it nervously. Maybe nobody would be home, and I could put this horrible conversation off for a while.

"Hello?" my mother answered.

"Mom. Hi, it's me," I said.

"Jessica? How are you, honey?" she asked. "Is everything all right?"

Every time I call home, Mom thinks something must be wrong. Unfortunately she was right this time.

"I'm not sick or anything, don't worry," I told her, flipping the business card over. "But . . ." I took a deep breath. "But I have some bad news."

"What is it, Jess? What's happened?"

"Well . . ." Oh, God, I really didn't want to do this. "Someone is in trouble."

"Who?" Mom's voice rose anxiously.

I kept staring at the back of the business card, where Lisa had written the day and time. I knew her handwriting so well. I knew *her* so well.

And I was about to betray her, after she begged me not to.

"Jessica," Mom said. "Are you there?"

"I'm here." I hesitated, still staring at my sister's handwriting. How could I say she was doing drugs when I didn't have a single bit of proof that she was? Okay, so she looked sick, but maybe she had the flu or something.

Erin said we should be sensible, and here I was jumping to one of the worst possible conclusions. And I was about to take Mom with me.

Did I really want to do that when I could be totally wrong about everything? Shouldn't I find out what was *really* going on first? Didn't I owe that to Lisa?

"Jessica, for heaven's sake, please tell me who's in trouble!" Mom insisted.

"Me," I blurted out. "It's me."

I'd decided not to tell her about Lisa, but I had to say something. And it was true, anyway. "I . . . um . . . threw a party in my room even though I wasn't supposed to. And I got caught. So now I'm on probation, which means I can't go anywhere on my own. And I'll have detention when we get back to Wisconsin."

I left out the juicy details like all the running up and down the halls and the wild music and hanging out in Alex's room until all hours. She didn't need to know *every*thing.

"You?" Mom gasped, sounding totally blown

away. "Probation? Detention? *You?*"

I guess I couldn't blame her for being so surprised. My friends were right—I wasn't much of a rule-breaker. "I'm sorry, Mom," I told her. "You would have found out when I got back, so I decided to break it to you now."

"I just can't believe you did such a thing, Jessica!" Now Mom sounded furious. "How could you? Don't you realize things like this might go on your high school record? It's a *permanent* record, you know."

"I know." She made me sound like a criminal. But I wasn't going to get in a fight with her. I kept quiet while she went on yelling at me. What could I say, anyway—"Hey, Mom, lighten up? I haven't been suspended, and detention won't go on my record. Besides, the party was fun?"

I was in enough trouble already.

As I listened to Mom with one ear, I kept fingering the Bliss card Lisa had dropped. *Friday*, she'd written on it. *6 P.M.*

Friday. Today. Lisa would be at Bliss at six P.M. today.

That was it, I decided. I'd give it one more try. I'd see if I could find her there and get her to tell me what was going on.

Of course, to get to Bliss I'd have to sneak out

of the hotel. What if I got caught?

Somehow it didn't really seem an issue anymore. This was for my sister. For Lisa. I'd just have to take the chance.

Chapter 9

Kerri

"**H**ow do I look?" I asked.

"Fine," Luke said.

"No. You look incredible," Matt said.

Maya rolled her eyes. "Kerri, you always look great. But right now you seem a little nervous. Tell yourself that you're really good at this. Act confident."

The four of us were standing in the hallway outside the Diamond Agency. Maya, Matt, and Luke had come along to give me moral support, which I definitely needed.

But I was the only one who could fight for a chance to prove myself. No wonder I looked a little nervous. A little? Try knee-shaking, heart-pounding, palm-sweating nervous!

"Okay, you can do this," I murmured to myself. I took a couple of deep breaths to relax. It didn't help, but I couldn't waste any more time. I glanced at the others. "I'm ready. Let's go."

We went through the big open doors into the agency's reception area, with its gilded furniture, thick mauve carpet, and silk fans on the walls.

It was the kind of posh place that could make almost anybody feel a little intimidated. Plus there were three other girls in the waiting area. Beautiful girls with high cheekbones and long legs and confident expressions on their flawless faces.

Fortunately I'd changed into a pair of black low-rise pants and a silky blue sweater. I couldn't exactly compete with experienced fashion models, but I thought I looked okay.

While my friends sat on one of the pink-upholstered couches, I walked confidently and elegantly—I hoped—to the front desk.

The receptionist glanced up from her computer. She was pretty elegant-looking herself, with big gray eyes and long, sleek dark hair.

"Hi, I'm Kerri Hopkins," I said. "I'd like to see Jane Katz. Is she in?"

She frowned slightly. "Do you have an appointment?"

"No, but I need to talk to her," I said. "It won't take long."

"I'm sorry, she won't see anyone without an appointment."

"Yes, but she already knows me," I told her. "I was in the contest at Marshall Fields. I left a message with her assistant yesterday. I guess she hasn't had a chance to call me back."

"I guess not," the woman agreed.

Pause. She was definitely not being helpful. "So could you please tell her I'm here?" I asked.

The phone buzzed. The receptionist picked it up, listened, then hung up. "Leslie Duval?" she called toward the couches. "You can go on back now."

One of the three models who'd been waiting stood up. She tossed her silky black hair over her shoulder, picked up her portfolio, and strode through the inner door.

The receptionist looked at me as if she'd forgotten why I was there.

"Could you let Jane know I'm here?" I reminded her. "It's important."

"I'm sure. But as I said, Ms. Katz won't see anyone without an appointment," the receptionist repeated. She turned back to her computer.

Great. I was being dismissed. For some reason, I hadn't expected that. But hey, why not? Jane Katz was obviously through with me.

As I stared through the doorway into the inner offices, a young woman wearing skinny reading glasses came out of one of the offices. She stopped, leaned against a wall, and started reading some papers on the clipboard she was carrying.

I realized I'd met her the first time I came to Diamond. She had interviewed me, and showed me to the agency reps. What was her name? Hannah, Hope? I couldn't remember. But maybe she could help me.

I waved, but Hannah or Hope didn't notice. I waved again.

The receptionist gave me a look that said, "Get lost."

I glanced over my shoulder. Matt and Luke made little "Keep going" motions with their hands. Maya frowned and lifted her chin toward the receptionist, mouthing the words, "Try again."

Right, I thought. I was glad they were there.

I cleared my throat. "Listen," I said to the receptionist. "I'd really appreciate it if you'd tell Ms. Katz I'm here. She sent me to the modeling contest, and I . . . well, it was kind of a disaster for me. But there was a very good reason. If I can just explain, I know she'll give me another chance."

The receptionist looked totally unconvinced. "I'm sure she'll return your call when she can," she said. "You can explain then."

"But I might be gone before she calls," I said. "I'm from Madison, Wisconsin, and I'm only here on a class trip. I'm leaving tomorrow afternoon. Can't you buzz her?"

The woman shook her head. She put her hand on the phone as if she was afraid I was going to pick it up and buzz Jane myself. Which wasn't a bad idea, except I didn't know her extension.

The phone rang again. The second model, with beautiful coppery skin and a long slender neck, was allowed into the inner sanctum.

I stared after her. Hannah or Hope was still there, making notes on her clipboard. I waved again, but she didn't seem to notice.

I was getting desperate. "Please," I begged. "Like I said, Jane knows me. She thinks I could be a really good model. I just need to talk to her. Please, it's so important."

"Look, she won't see you," the receptionist declared. "Now if you want to make an appointment, I can try to set one up. But there's no way you'll get in today."

The woman was obviously made of stone. Even though I stood there for a few more seconds, she typed on her computer, answered the phone, and shot a couple of suspicious glances at Maya and Luke and Matt. But she never once glanced at me again.

I felt totally invisible.

And totally crushed. It was over. This was my last chance, and I didn't make it happen.

I spun around. My friends got up, but I was too upset to say anything to them just then. I walked quickly out of the reception area and down the hall to the elevators.

I felt Matt's arm go around my shoulders. "Hey, Kerri, you gave it your best shot," he murmured.

"Yeah, I would have buzzed you in a flash," Luke agreed.

"I couldn't believe that receptionist," Maya added, punching the down arrow. "Talk about harsh!"

I just nodded. If I tried to talk, I'd start sobbing right there in the hallway. I really, really didn't want to do that.

The elevator arrived, and the doors opened. As we were getting on, a voice called out, "Hold the elevator, please!"

Matt pushed the Open Door button, and we all waited. In a couple of seconds, Hannah or Hope came running in, her long braids bouncing up and down.

"Thanks," she said breathlessly.

"Heidi," I said as the elevator started down. "That's your name, right?"

She nodded. "Heidi Snyder. I know you too. We

met at the open call."

"Yes. I'm Kerri Hopkins."

"That's right. Listen, I overheard you talking to Marilyn."

Marilyn? Oh. The receptionist, I figured.

"I know. I saw you," I told her. "Is she always that helpful?"

Heidi smiled. "She's just doing her job. Anyway, she's right. You can't get to Jane. It's too bad too. I saw you work it at the Marshall Fields contest. You have a great look, and you're obviously ambitious. I don't think you should give up."

That was all I needed to hear. "I don't plan on giving up," I said. Even though I wasn't sure what to do next. "Maybe you can help me. Are you a booker?"

Heidi nodded again. "Associate booker. But I work for Jane. I can't help you either, well, not officially."

"What about unofficially?" I was being pushy, but at this point I had nothing to lose. "I mean, you must know other modeling agencies. Other bookers. Couldn't you give me a name?"

Heidi hesitated, biting her lip.

"Please?" I asked.

"I could get in a lot of trouble," she told me. "I'm not supposed to help the competition."

"But Jane doesn't want me," I argued. "I'm free to go to anybody I want. I just need a name, that's all."

Heidi thought for a second. Then she reached into her pants pocket and pulled out a slim metal case. She opened it and pulled out a business card. It was for a modeling agency called Hightower, with the name Rachel Santos printed underneath.

"Rachel's a booker," Heidi explained. "She's also a friend of mine, and I think she'll see you. But I heard you say you're leaving tomorrow, so it'll have to be tonight."

The elevator stopped. The doors opened, and Heidi hurried into the lobby. "Hightower is across town, and it closes in half an hour," she called back over her shoulder. "You'll have to hurry. Good luck."

"Thank you!" I called after her as the rest of us got off the elevator. "Thanks a lot!"

"Whoa, Kerri, that was awesome," Matt said, giving me a hug. "I couldn't believe the way you got that name out of her."

I laughed, feeling a little giddy. I could hardly believe it myself. Maybe I had a chance after all.

Chapter 10

Jessica

When Erin came back to our room, I was standing at the mirror brushing a tiny bit of sparkle shadow onto my eyelids.

"Let's see," Erin said, checking me out. "Short skirt, black tank top, eye glitter. Just let me take a quick shower, and I'll be out of here."

"What are you talking about?" I uncapped a tube of cinnamon-colored lipstick and started putting it on.

"Well, Alex is coming, right?" she asked. "I should disappear so you guys can have some privacy."

I shook my head. "I'm not getting dressed for Alex."

"Oh. So this the new look for girls who are on probation and can't leave their hotel rooms?" Erin asked with a sly smile.

"No." I capped the lipstick. "It's the look for

girls on probation who are sneaking out of their hotel rooms."

Erin's eyes widened. "Jessica, are you kidding me?"

"Nope. I'm going to Bliss. I have to find Lisa," I said. I checked myself in the mirror. I looked nervous, probably because I was. Very nervous. But I had to do this. "How's the outfit?" I asked Erin. "How's the makeup?"

"You look great, but Jess!" Erin plopped down on the bed, staring at me. "First you throw the party, then you sneak away from Navy Pier. Now you're actually going to sneak out of the hotel? Don't you think you're pushing your luck right about now?"

"Definitely," I agreed. "But I'm not doing it for fun, Erin. Okay, throwing the party was, but this isn't. Lisa might be in serious trouble."

I checked my makeup again, then started brushing my hair. Lisa had written 6 *P.M.* on the card. I didn't have much time.

"Why don't you call the club?" Erin suggested.

"I tried that about ten times already. It's always busy," I replied. "Besides, I decided that talking to her on the phone won't do any good. She could just hang up on me or something. I have to see her in person."

"Yeah. I guess that makes sense."

"So will you cover for me?" I asked as I stuffed my wallet and a comb into my black shoulder bag. "I know it's not fair, because you could get in trouble too, but—"

"But it's important so I'll chance it," Erin told me. "Just leave Ms. Gomes to me."

"You're the best, Erin." I leaned down and gave her a quick hug. "I knew I could count on you. Thanks."

"Hey, you'd do it for me," Erin said. She hopped off the bed and went to the door. "Coast is clear," she announced as she peered out. "You go to the elevator. I'll hang out by Ms. Gomes's room. If she comes out while you're waiting, I'll keep her busy until you're gone."

"How will you do that?" I asked, taking my jean jacket off the back of the chair.

Erin shrugged. "I'll ask her advice about something, like . . . what kind of souvenir I should get my parents."

"Nobody asks Ms. Gomes's advice about anything but calculus," I pointed out.

"That's why it'll work," Erin declared. "She'll be so glad to be asked, she'll talk for hours. No, wait, I'd die of boredom. Okay, never mind. I'll think of something."

Erin stuck her head out again. "Still clear," she said, pulling the door all the way open. "Go for it, Jess!"

Five minutes later, I climbed into a cab and told the driver where I wanted to go. "I have to be there by six," I said, checking my watch. We only had twelve minutes. "Do you think we can make it?"

"No problem." The driver started the meter, hit the gas, and pulled away fast enough to pin me against the backseat.

Great. I might get there by six, but would I get there alive?

After a minute, though, I stopped worrying about the ride and started thinking about other things. Like what if Ms. Gomes suddenly decided to keep a close watch on Erin and me again? What would I say if Lisa really was into drugs? What would I say, period? Would she even be there?

Once I'd made up my mind to sneak out, I'd just plowed ahead without really thinking. All of a sudden I felt extremely unsure about the whole thing.

"Four minutes to spare," the driver announced, swerving hard to the right. "Not bad, huh?" he added with a glance over his shoulder.

It took a second to realize that he'd pulled over to the curb. Then I saw the sign on the outside of the building. The name Bliss wrote itself over and over in purple-neon script.

I thanked the driver and paid him, then stood outside the club for a few seconds. It was a low cinder-block building. No windows, just a big double door with an awning that ran out to the sidewalk.

While I was standing there, a bunch of kids trooped across the street and headed for the door. They looked a little older than me. College, maybe. I scanned their faces, but Lisa wasn't one of them. Maybe she'd gotten here early.

I followed the kids through the door. A sign just inside said the place was for people sixteen and over. I dug out my wallet and showed my driver's license to a girl in black jeans and a white shirt with Bliss stitched in purple across the back. She checked my ID and waved me on.

There was a bar up front, but the rest of the place was wide open for dancing. Well, almost wide open. A bunch of large podiums were placed around the floor. They had wide, round flat tops like café tables, but they were too high for chairs. Maybe people stood at them to drink or something.

The place was really cool, with revolving mirrored globes, strobe lights, and pounding music blasting over the speakers. Maybe Lisa was meeting some friends here. Or a guy.

She wasn't sitting at the bar. And there weren't very many people on the dance floor yet, so it was easy to see that she wasn't there either.

Maybe she knew somebody who worked here.

I decided to go ask the girl who'd checked my ID. On my way, I ran into a guy wearing black jeans and a Bliss shirt. He had a thick neck, wide shoulders, and a suspicious gaze. Probably a bouncer on the lookout for trouble.

The music was so loud I had to shout at him. "Excuse me! Do you know Lisa Carvelli?"

He cupped his ear. "What?"

I took a deep breath. "Lisa Carvelli!"

"Oh! Hey, you showed up!" he hollered back, looking surprised.

Great. He thought *I* was Lisa. Wait—it *was* great! That meant he knew her. "No, I'm—"

"Good thing too!" he shouted. "We don't like to come up short. Terry was pretty pissed since it's your first night. Come on!"

Before I could explain or ask any questions, the guy was striding toward a door at the far end of the bar. I hurried to keep up. "The place is pretty quiet right now," he bellowed over his shoulder.

Quiet? I thought.

"It'll fill up soon, though. We've got some

music people coming in early for an album-launching party. Good luck!" He threw open the door, gestured me through it, and left without looking inside.

No wonder. It was a dressing room, and a couple of the girls inside were in the middle of changing clothes. Others were sitting at dressing tables, putting on makeup or brushing their hair. They were all young. Nineteen or so. One of them must have just finished telling a joke, because they were all laughing.

They smiled at me when I came in. I smiled back, feeling very nervous.

"Welcome to the madhouse," one of the girls said. She had curly red hair and lots of freckles and a friendly grin.

"Thanks."

"Don't scare her," another girl said. "It's not a madhouse. It's just a little chaotic, that's all."

The redhead laughed. "Same thing." She stood up and patted my shoulder as she headed for the door. "But it's fun."

I found an empty space at one of the makeup tables and sat down. Now what? Well, everybody seemed nice. I should just ask about Lisa.

Before I could say anything, one of the girls who'd been changing clothes suddenly noticed me.

She finished buttoning her billowy purple shirt as she walked over. "That's supposed to be Lisa's place," she declared, crossing her arms and narrowing her blue eyes at me. "And you're obviously not her. So where is she?"

"I . . . I'm Jessica," I said. "Jessica Carvelli—Lisa's sister."

"No kidding?" The girl's expression brightened all of a sudden. "Oh, I get it!"

Get what? I wondered.

"It's really cool that you're doing this for her," she went on. "I mean, Terry was going to fire her for calling in sick on her first night, and I know she needs the money. I'm Jenna, by the way."

"Hi," I said. I was glad Jenna was happy, but I still didn't have a clue what she was talking about. "Listen, I—"

"I'm so relieved you're here, you just don't know," Jenna went on, running her fingers through her long blond hair. "I mean, I really stuck my neck out for Lisa, getting her this job and everything. I mean, we've got a special party coming. Terry was all ready to blame me, and I can't afford to get fired either."

I only had about a zillion questions. Terry was probably the owner or the manager; that much I could figure out. But what about Lisa? Did Jenna know where she was living? Why did she need money so badly? And if she did, why would she call in sick on her first night of work?

But before I could start interrogating Jenna, somebody banged on the door. "We're starting to fill up!" a man's voice called out. "Time to get moving!"

"Okay, let's go. Your jacket and purse will be safe in here," Jenna said. She grabbed my arm and pulled me toward the door with the rest of the girls, who were hurrying out.

Back on the dance floor, Jenna dropped my arm and plunged into the crowd. The music was blasting, and she didn't hear me when I called out to her.

I stood there feeling abandoned and confused. What was I supposed to do? Maybe I should go wait at the bar or something. No, I couldn't do that. They'd think Lisa hadn't shown up, and they'd fire her.

Then a dark-haired girl I'd seen in the dressing room nudged me in the arm and leaned close to my ear. "You're up there," she said. She was pointing at one of the flat-topped podiums.

Huh?

I glanced around and noticed that not all the podiums were empty. People were dancing on top of them. Jenna was on one. The curly redhead was on another. Two of the podiums had guys on them, and three more girls I'd seen in the dressing room were on others.

So this was Lisa's job. And I was supposed to take her place. To get up on a podium and dance in front of a bunch of complete strangers.

I couldn't do this. Erin would love it. Kerri probably would too. But I would just die of embarrassment.

I guess I looked totally panicked, because the dark-haired girl grinned. "Don't worry. After five minutes, you'll forget all about everybody else," she said. "Just have fun with it."

Fun? I didn't think so. It would be more like torture.

But I knew I had to do it. After all, it was for Lisa. She'd already lost the job at the boutique. I didn't want her to lose another one, not if she really needed it. I'd get her address from Jenna as soon as possible, but in the meantime, I had to help my sister out.

I walked over to the podium and found four steps leading up the back. I climbed them to the top. The music was pounding. The dance floor was packed. Colored strobe lights swept across the crowd's faces, turning them red and orange and green and purple.

Everyone seemed to be staring up at me.

I felt like jumping down and running away as fast as I could.

But this was my only lead to Lisa. If I wanted to find her, I couldn't run away.

So I started to dance.

Chapter 11

Kerri

"**W**hy didn't I pay attention in that class on the power of crystals my mom dragged me to last year?" I muttered as Maya, Luke, Matt, and I stood on the El platform. "Maybe if I was holding crystal it would make the train come faster."

My mother was heavily into New Age stuff like astrology, feng shui, and meditation. When she divorced my dad seven years ago, and we moved into our apartment, we had to put dishes of salt in every corner to ward off evil.

Until about ten minutes ago, I thought it was all a crock. Now I wasn't so sure.

We only had fifteen more minutes to get to the Hightower Agency. "Plenty of time," the man at the train station said. "It's only two stops."

Of course, we had to get on the train first.

"Mom's always reciting some mantra or other," I declared. "And I bet she knows one for lifting the curse on late trains!"

"Try not to think about it, Kerri," Maya told me. "It just makes it seem longer."

"Right. Okay." I stopped talking, and tried to empty my mind.

No one said anything for a few minutes.

"I can't stand this waiting!" I burst out.

"Maybe we should forget the train and take a cab," Matt said.

"It's rush hour," Luke reminded him. "Getting a cab will be tough."

Luke was right, unfortunately. It was so frustrating! This fabulous chance to see another modeling agent might actually slip away because I couldn't get to her in time!

Come on, come on, come on, I silently chanted. *Come on, come on!*

"Hey!" Matt held up his hand. "Do you hear that?"

We all froze, listening. A rumble in the distance grew louder and louder. A whistle shrieked, and the train clattered into view.

"There *is* a God!' I cried.

Maya laughed. "Don't lose it now, Kerri. We're going to make it."

The train screeched to a stop. We had to squeeze in like sardines because it was so crowded, but it didn't matter. At least we were on our way.

The train lurched forward, pulled out of the station, began to pick up speed . . . and stopped.

Everyone in the car was silent. Waiting. A pager beeped. A newspaper rustled. Someone coughed.

The train didn't move.

I couldn't believe this. I wanted to scream, but I probably would have gotten arrested for starting a stampede.

People started murmuring. Some of them grumbled. Some made jokes about the transit system.

"I don't see anything funny about a broken-down train," I said to Matt. He was standing right behind me with one arm around my waist.

"It's probably just a short delay," he said, pressing his arm a little tighter.

"Don't count on it," a man's voice advised sarcastically. "I sat on a stalled train for an hour on this line the other day."

An hour! I let out a groan. I leaned against Matt and squeezed my eyes shut. If the train didn't get moving soon, I was afraid I'd flip out. I desperately tried not to count the seconds, but I couldn't stop myself.

I lost track somewhere around two hundred,

so I don't know exactly how long it was. But the train finally gave a jerk and began to roll again.

I didn't dare look at my watch. If we were late, I didn't want to know it.

When the train reached our stop, we squeezed out and raced downstairs to the street. Luke found Lincoln Avenue on his map. "One block over," he said. "What's the address?"

I checked the business card. "Five fifty-seven. Hurry!"

We ran to the corner of Lincoln Avenue and were halfway up the block when Maya suddenly stopped. "I hate to tell you, but the numbers are going down."

Could anything else go wrong?

Matt grabbed my hand, pulled me around, and we headed in the opposite direction. I was beyond screaming. I was beyond groaning. All I could do was run. And hope we made it in time. I couldn't lose this chance. I just couldn't.

We finally got to the right address and hurried inside. Hightower was on the sixth floor. We piled into an elevator, and I finally got up the nerve to look at my watch.

We were eight minutes late. But I wasn't going to quit now.

The elevator stopped on the sixth floor.

Hightower was directly across the hall. Its door was open, and I could see a receptionist sitting at her desk.

"We made it, Kerri!" Maya declared, giving me a little hug. "Now go for it."

Matt kissed my cheek and smiled at me. I combed my fingers through my hair and took a deep breath. I gave myself a quick pep talk—*Be confident, believe in yourself, you can do it*—and walked through the door.

The others followed me and sat down in some chairs in the waiting area. Hightower had gone for the Minimalist look—black leather chairs, chrome-and-glass tables, track lighting. No soft cushions or thick carpet. The only color in the place came from the framed magazine covers of models.

I thought it was classy. Maybe a little cold. But the receptionist was much friendlier than the one at Diamond. Unfortunately, she basically said the same thing—I couldn't get in to see the agent.

"Ms. Santos is on the phone right now. A conference call," she explained. "And the office is about to close for the day. Why don't you come back another time?"

"I can't," I told her. "I don't live in Chicago. And I'm leaving tomorrow. This is the only time I can see her."

She smiled sympathetically. "I'm sorry. I wish I could help, but I can't." She started shuffling papers into neat stacks and putting pens and paper clips away.

I went back to the others. "I guess you heard," I said.

Maya nodded. "It just isn't fair."

"Yeah, but what's Kerri supposed to do?" Luke asked. "She can't just plow past the receptionist."

Matt put his arm around me and pulled me aside. "You okay?" he murmured.

"Umm." Actually, I wasn't really listening. I was thinking about what Luke said. He was right—I couldn't plow past the receptionist, but . . .

"Listen, I know how much you want this, but it seems like it's just not going to happen this trip," Matt told me. "But it's not over for good, Kerri. Right?"

"Right. It's definitely not over for good." I smiled at him. "Let me just use the bathroom and then we can go."

I hurried back to Maya. "Bathroom," I said, grabbing her arm.

Maya looked surprised, but she didn't argue. It was easy to get the receptionist to take pity on us and give us the bathroom key. "Down that hall to the end and make a right," she said, pointing to a doorway behind her.

"Thanks!" I practically pushed Maya through the door. "Okay. Here's the plan," I announced in a low whisper.

"What plan?" Maya demanded. "What's going on, Kerri?"

"Look. I can't just turn around and walk out of here without trying everything," I told her. "If I go back to Madison without an agent, I might never have another shot at big-time modeling. So it's now or never."

"Then I guess it's now," Maya agreed. "Okay. What's the plan? What do you want me to do?"

"Help me find Rachel Santos's office," I said. "I'll take it from there."

For the next few minutes, Maya and I scurried through the halls of the Hightower Agency, checking nameplates on doors. Most of the offices were already empty. But according to the receptionist, Ms. Santos was on the phone. As long as she was here, I still had a chance.

"There it is," Maya whispered as she pointed to a nameplate that said *Rachel Santos*. The door to her office was open just a crack.

I stepped closer and listened. "I can't hear anything," I whispered.

Maya leaned close. "I do. Papers or something.

Good, she's probably off the phone." She squeezed my arm.

I reached out to push the door open and suddenly stopped. Could I really do this?

"Kerri?" Maya murmured. "What are you waiting for?"

"I'm scared," I confessed. "What if she kicks me out?"

"You won't be any worse off than you are now," Maya whispered. "But like you said, this is a chance you can't throw away. You have to take this as far as you can, or you'll never be happy. Besides, Kerri, you're a fabulous model, and you're going to do great. Go for it!"

Maya was right. I had to go for it. What did I have to lose?

I smoothed my sweater, shook my hair back, straightened up, and pushed the door wide open. "Ms. Santos?"

The woman behind the desk jumped in surprise and dropped the pile of photographs she was holding. "Who are you?" she demanded.

Chapter 12

Jessica

With the music pounding like a heartbeat, I spun around on the platform, swayed from side to side, then spun around again.

Cheers and clapping rose around me like a wave. Lights flashed across the faces of the crowd, and as I gazed down, I saw that people were smiling up at me. Clapping and shouting.

For me.

I laughed. I spun around again, raising my arms and letting myself really get into it. I don't know how long I'd been dancing, but I finally realized that this was a total trip. Amazing. Whoever thought I'd actually enjoy it?

At first I'd had to keep reminding myself to just move my feet. It felt weird not dancing *with* someone. It felt extremely weird dancing on a platform above a crowd of strangers. It was like being on display. Which I was, and I didn't like it.

112

But now I realized it wasn't like a contest or anything. The people on the floor were dancing too, and they cheered and clapped for everyone on the platforms.

I knew it didn't matter what I did as long as I danced.

I danced in a little circle around the platform, shaking my hips and clapping my hands, smiling down at the kids below.

It was as though I had let the music inside me, and I could feel my body loosen up. All of a sudden it was a rush to be up there above a sea of laughing, dancing, shouting people.

Maybe Kerri got this feeling when she was cheerleading and all the fans stamped their feet and shouted with her. Maybe this was what it was like to sing at a rock concert and have thousands of kids screaming and reaching for you.

Okay, I was getting carried away. *Time to come back down to earth, Jess,* I told myself. But the energy in the place was catching, and I didn't even feel tired when another dancer came and told me to take a break.

"The break room's next to the dressing room," she told me as I climbed off the platform. "You've got about twenty minutes. Put your feet up and relax."

"Thanks." My adrenaline was still pumping, and I didn't feel tired at all. But I definitely wanted something to drink. Gallons of something.

I made my way through the crowd and got my bag and jacket from the dressing room. Then I went into the break room. There were a couple of fat couches and some easy chairs arranged around a coffee table piled with magazines. A soda machine, a coffee maker, and a candy machine stood against one of the walls.

A guy and two girls were sitting on a sofa and talking. One of the girls was the dark-haired one who showed me which platform to dance on.

The freckle-faced redheaded girl from the dressing room was in an easy chair, knitting something out of cherry-red yarn. A second guy was feeding coins into the candy machine.

Jenna wasn't there. Didn't she get a break too? I hoped she'd be in soon so I could talk to her.

Everyone glanced at me when I came in. "Hi, how's it going?" the dark-haired girl asked.

"Okay, I think," I told her. "It's the first time I've done this."

"Really?" The redhead looked up from her knitting with a smile. "I saw you out there—you're a natural."

"Thanks." *A natural, huh?* I thought with a

grin. Maybe I had hidden talents.

"Yeah, you looked great," she said. "I'm Amy, by the way. So how do you like it?"

"I love it." I laughed. It really *was* amazing. "I've never done anything like it. I'm having so much fun."

"It is fun, isn't it?" Amy agreed. "See, Derrick?" she said to the guy at the candy machine. "You're the only one who doesn't like it."

"That's because I'm the only one with any brains." Derrick tore the wrapping from a Hershey Bar and grinned at me. "I'm kidding. It's a great job, and I'm earning good money for school. But I have to work until closing tonight, so I had to cancel a date."

"You actually had a date?" one of the other girls teased.

Derrick threw his candy wrapper at her.

I smiled. Everyone was so friendly, and the dancing was so exciting. I could see why Lisa would want a job like this. Still, I didn't know why she actually needed a job like this. Or any job here in Chicago.

Except she might not have this job if it wasn't for me, I reminded myself. *She called in sick, remember? She would have been fired if I hadn't shown up.*

Then I wondered if she was really sick, like with the flu, or was she sick because of drugs? I shook it out of my mind. Concentrate on finding her first, I thought.

"Sit down," Amy told me. "Relax before your next set. You look kind of hot."

"I am," I said, pulling my hair up off my neck. "I've got to drink something first, though. My mouth feels like a desert."

I got a bottle of water from the soda machine and took a long drink.

I was about to ask the others if they knew Lisa when the bouncer opened the door and stuck his head in. "There you are," he said to me. "Terry asked me to find you."

Oh, no. Did the manager figure out I wasn't Lisa?

The bouncer handed me a sheet of paper. "You left some information off your employee form. You can fill out the rest while you're here and give it back to me before you leave tonight."

"Oh. Okay, sure." As the bouncer left, I quickly scanned the form. There was Lisa's name and social security number. She'd left the phone number and the emergency contact boxes blank. But she'd filled in the address.

1117 Hill Street, Apt. 2A, Chicago.

I'd found her! I knew where she lived. I could go see her and find out if she was all right. Make her tell me what was going on.

I glanced up. "Is there a phone somewhere?" I asked.

"There's a pay phone up by the bar, but it's way too noisy out there," Amy said. She fished around in her knitting bag and pulled out a cell phone. "Use this."

"Thanks." I took the phone and called my hotel room. Erin answered on the first ring.

"Jess!" she said, sounding a little frazzled. "I thought you'd never call!"

"Sorry, I got kind of busy. But guess what?" I said. "I found Lisa."

"Really? What's going on with her?"

"I don't know, I haven't seen her yet." I explained about finding the address. "Listen, I have to dance some more, but—"

"Wait a sec," Erin interrupted. "Did you say you have to dance?"

"It's a long story. I'll tell you everything when I get back," I promised. "But I'm so excited about finding Lisa. I'm going to go see her tonight."

"Not a good idea," Erin said. "I don't blame you for wanting to, but I'm not sure I can hold Ms. Gomes off much longer. She's already knocked on our door three times, and I'm running out of excuses. We're heading for big trouble, Jess. Capital B, Capital T."

"Okay, you're right," I told her. My risking suspension was one thing, but I couldn't ask Erin to do it too. "I'll come back as soon as I can," I promised. "I'll go see Lisa first thing in the morning. If Ms. Gomes knocks again, just don't answer. Put the DO NOT DISTURB sign on the door."

"Yeah, maybe she'll think we're both asleep," Erin agreed. "It's worth a try. But hurry."

Erin sounded slightly panicky, and I didn't blame her. She was the only one standing between us and major trouble. But I'd finally found my sister. And I had to go see her, even if it meant sneaking away again tomorrow.

Kerri

"Who are you?" the woman repeated. Her brown eyes stared at me suspiciously from behind oval silver-framed glasses.

"My name is Kerri Hopkins," I replied. "I'm sorry for barging in on you. You *are* Rachel Santos, aren't you?" I wanted to make sure.

She nodded. "I know the name of everybody who works here, and Kerri Hopkins isn't one of them. I also know Eileen wouldn't send you back without telling me." She reached for the telephone.

"Please wait," I said quickly. "Heidi Snyder gave me your card. She told me to come see you."

"I'll bet she didn't tell you to pop in without being announced," Ms. Santos said. Her hand tightened on the phone.

"No, that was my idea," I admitted. "And I'm sorry. I wouldn't have done it except . . . I had to."

Ms. Santos didn't say anything, but she didn't pick up the phone and call security either.

This was it. My last chance before I had to leave Chicago. I took a deep breath and started talking.

I told her about the Diamond Agency, about Donna and how she ruined the modeling contest for me. I said the Diamond Agency wouldn't give me another chance, but I thought I deserved it.

"I'm good," I declared. "I know I don't have a lot of experience, but I learn fast. This trip was really important, and it's almost over. I can't make appointments to see agents next week or next month. I'm leaving town tomorrow afternoon. That's why I sneaked in here to see you. I couldn't leave without trying one more time. As long as there was a chance, I had to take it."

When I finished, Ms. Santos folded her arms

and leaned back in her chair, staring at me.

I just stood there. I didn't know what else to say. I was totally talked out.

Finally she pushed her glasses up and reached for a pad and pencil. "Okay," she said.

"Okay?" I repeated. But what did that mean? *Okay, I listened, now get out?*

"You've got plenty of drive, I'll give you that," she told me, scribbling on the pad. "There's a lot of talent around, but talent doesn't always mean success. Most of the time you have to make it happen."

I didn't catch on at first until she ripped off the sheet of paper and handed it to me. "That's my photographer's studio address," she said. "I'll call Tom and tell him you'll be there tomorrow morning to get some pictures taken. It's Saturday, and he only works until noon. Be there at ten o'clock sharp."

My stomach did a complete flip. "You mean . . . does this mean you're hiring me?"

"No. It depends on the photos," she said. "If they're good, we'll talk. Otherwise . . ." She shrugged.

Otherwise, forget it. That's what she meant. But the photos would definitely be good. I'd make sure of that.

"This is so great!" I told her. "I can't believe it. Thank you."

She smiled and peered at me over the top of her glasses. "Like I said, you obviously have the drive to succeed. And you have a good commercial look. But hundreds of girls get their photos taken every year. Only a handful get chosen. Keep that in mind."

I nodded. But at the moment the only thing in my mind was that I'd done it! I'd made another chance for myself.

And from now on nothing—and no one—was going to mess it up.

Chapter 13

"Here she is!" Matt sang out as we pranced through the lobby of the office building. "Famous Hightower model . . . Kerrriii Hopkins!"

Maya clapped. Luke whistled and cheered.

The elevator doors opened. Matt grabbed my hand and began to dance with me across the lobby. Everyone turned and stared.

"You're looking at a future cover girl!" Matt announced. "Everyone told her she couldn't do it, but would she take no for an answer? No way!"

"Matt, this is totally embarrassing," I said. But I didn't stop smiling.

I *couldn't* stop smiling, not that I really wanted to. I was so excited when I left Ms. Santos's office I could hardly speak.

"She's actually sending you to a professional photographer?" Maya kept saying over and over. "That is so awesome, Kerri!"

I waved the piece of paper with the studio's address. "Tomorrow," I managed to say. "Ten in the morning. Thank God the buses aren't leaving until noon. It's going to be tight, but I'll make it."

Matt whooped and lifted me off the floor in a big hug. Luke patted my back, and Maya kept saying, "I knew you could do it. I knew you could do it!"

We celebrated all the way back to the hotel. We stopped and ate pizza, then stopped at another place for ice cream. Then we finally headed back.

The others rode the train. I floated.

I was still floating when we got back to the hotel. I didn't know if I'd ever come down. I couldn't wait to find Erin and Jess and tell them everything.

Matt danced me into a waiting elevator. Luke and Maya got on behind us. When it stopped at Maya's and my floor, I gave Matt a quick kiss on the cheek. "Thanks a lot for sticking by me today," I told him.

"Anytime," he said. He cupped his hand against the side of my face and smiled. "All the time."

Maya grinned at me as we got out and the elevator door closed. "Matt really knows how to say things, doesn't he? Not that he doesn't mean it," she added quickly. "He's just got the right words."

"Mmm," I agreed. "The right moves too."

"Oh, really?" Maya raised an eyebrow. "You want to tell me about it?"

"You're not old enough," I teased. Maya was a year younger than the rest of our group.

"Very funny."

"Kerri, Maya!" Erin called out from the other end of the hall. She was in her leopard-print slippers and the red kimono she always wore as a robe. "I was just coming to find you. Wait till you hear what Jess did."

"Wait till you hear what Kerri did," Maya told her.

"What *about* Jess?" I asked. I remembered how upset she'd looked at the play, but I hadn't had a chance to talk to her. "Did she find out something awful about Lisa? Is she in trouble with Ms. Gomes again?"

Erin shook her head no. "She's back, and she's taking a shower."

"Back? You mean she left the hotel?" Maya asked. "Is she getting to like living dangerously?"

"Not so loud," Erin whispered. "Ms. Gomes might be lurking around the corner. Let's go into your room, and I'll tell you everything."

Once we got inside our room, Erin filled us in

on all the details of Jess's adventure.

"It's kind of hard to picture Jess up on a platform dancing in front of hundreds of people," I said. "I guess we can't tease her anymore about never doing anything exciting."

"So what happened with you, Kerri?" Erin asked. "I can tell it's good news—you look totally happy."

"I have an appointment for a photo session tomorrow," I announced. "With a completely different modeling agency."

"Kerri, that's so great!" Erin hugged me. "How did you do it?"

Maya and I took turns telling her the whole story, about the snobby receptionist and Heidi Snyder, the stuck train, sneaking into the Hightower offices—and finally finding Rachel Santos.

"I thought for sure she was going to kick me out, so I talked as fast as I could," I said. "I can't even remember everything I told her, but I guess it worked. I still can't believe it."

I let out a big sigh and flopped onto my bed. I glanced at the phone on the nightstand. Its light was blinking. *Could it be Jane Katz?* I wondered with a smile. *Oh, well. Too late for her.* But I still wanted to hear what she had to say.

I picked up the phone and punched the message button.

Donna's voice spoke in a rush of words. "Kerri-it's-Donna-don't-hang-up."

I almost did. But she sounded different somehow. Quiet and kind of serious. Maybe she was going to apologize for the earlier phone call. Maybe she'd finally gotten her act together.

"I know you don't trust me," Donna said.

No kidding, I thought.

"I guess I can't blame you," Donna went on. "But I have to talk to you. It's really important. There's a Starbucks across the street from your hotel, at the end of the block. Please meet me there at nine tomorrow. It'll be busy, and you'll feel safe. You need to hear what I have to say. If you come, I promise it'll be the last time you ever see me."

Click. The message was over.

I hung up and stared at the phone. I hadn't exactly forgotten Donna, but I'd shoved her way to the back of my mind while I was out trying to save my modeling career.

All of a sudden, she was right up front again. Why couldn't she just leave me alone? Every time something good happened, Donna popped up and spoiled it.

"Who was that?" Maya asked.

"My friendly neighborhood stalker."

"Oh, no," Maya groaned. "What did she want? As if I don't know."

"She wants to talk," I said. "She asked me to meet her tomorrow at that Starbucks across the street. You know why she picked that place? She said I'd feel safe there."

Erin rolled her eyes. "The girl is definitely deluded. Like you'd feel safe *any*where near her."

"She said she has something important to tell me, and then she'll stop bugging me." I knew I shouldn't believe her. And I didn't, not really. Still, she *did* sound different. Not threatening or anything. What did she want to tell me? "She practically begged me to come," I added.

"Well, too bad," Maya declared. "How can she expect you to meet her? She's psycho!"

"Don't go anywhere near that Starbucks tomorrow," Erin warned me. "Don't even walk on that side of the street."

"Yeah, you're right," I agreed. "Besides, she wants to meet me at nine, and I have to be at the studio at ten. There's no way I'm going to let her make me miss that photo shoot."

As I got up to undress, I noticed that the phone light was still blinking. I hadn't erased Donna's message yet.

"It'll be the last time you ever see me," she'd said.

She'd sounded almost sorry. And she was so calm and quiet that I couldn't help wondering if she really meant it. If I listened to what Donna had to say, would that really get her out of my life for good?

Jessica

"Hey, Jess, where are you going?"

Alex's voice stopped me as I hurried through the lobby the next morning.

I was caught. But at least it wasn't by Ms. Gomes.

I turned around. Alex was standing near the door of the hotel coffee shop, looking a little sleepy-eyed.

"It's only eight-thirty," I said, as he walked over to me. "What are you doing up so early?"

"I kept dreaming that somebody was moving the furniture," he yawned. "Turned out to be my roommate snoring. It went on all night. I got about two hours of sleep. I need coffee."

"Sounds good." I smiled and started to edge away from him. I hadn't seen any teachers around yet, but I was definitely pushing my luck.

Alex caught my hand. "This is our last day in

Chicago—want to have breakfast with me?"

"I would love to, but I can't," I told him. "I . . . um . . ." I had to think of a good excuse.

"You have to sneak out of the hotel, fast," he said.

Caught again. "How did you know that?"

"Hey, I'm sleepy, not blind," he said. "The look on your face is a dead giveaway. Plus the way you were glancing over your shoulder while you scurried across the lobby."

I had to smile. He made me sound like a fugitive. I guess I was. "Okay, you're right," I admitted. "But I have to get out of here, Alex. I found out where Lisa's living, and I'm going there now."

"No kidding? That's great, Jess. That you found the address, I mean."

"Right, and I'm going to see her," I said. "I just hope she's there. It's my last chance before we leave."

Alex frowned. "I suppose so, but . . ."

"Don't tell me. I'm breaking probation," I declared. "I know I am."

"Okay, I won't tell you what you already know," he said.

"Why don't you come with me?" I suddenly asked. "I'm a little nervous. I mean, I don't know what I'll find when I get to her house." I knew I could count on Alex to be calm no matter what happened. Calm and sensible, that was Alex. And I might need someone like that.

Alex hesitated.

"You won't get in trouble or anything," I added. "If Ms. Gomes finds out I left, I won't tell her you were with me."

"I wasn't thinking about that," he said. "I'm just worried about *you* getting in trouble."

That was Alex too, I thought. Sweet enough to worry about me. But maybe he didn't understand how important this was.

"I have to go, Alex," I said. "I don't have a lot of time, and I can't leave town without talking to Lisa. I just can't."

He nodded. "I guess you know what you're doing. Let me check my money situation." He pulled out his wallet and looked inside. Then he grabbed my hand. "Okay. Let's go."

After a twenty-minute train ride and a ten-minute walk in a run-down neighborhood near the University of Chicago, Alex and I found Lisa's address on Hill Street.

Hers was narrow three-story building. The door opened onto a tiny vestibule with a chipped tile floor. It wasn't just chipped, it was filthy. The walls were tiled too. At least they had been, once upon a time. Half the tiles were missing.

Alex and I squeezed inside. "What's that smell?" he asked.

"I don't want to know," I replied. I shuddered a little. Why was Lisa living in a place like this?

There were six mailboxes on one of the walls. Only half of them had names, and none of them was Lisa's. The name on 2A was missing. Alex was about to press the buzzer above it when I noticed that the inner door was partly open.

"Let's just go up," I told him. "Lisa was acting so weird when I saw her, I'm afraid she might tell me to get lost. She might not, if we're face-to-face."

We went inside and started up a dark narrow stairway toward the second floor. The farther I climbed, the more I wanted to turn around and run back out.

The mysterious odor had disappeared, but now I smelled old grease and rotting garbage. The stairway was actually pulling away from the wall, which had old, stained wallpaper peeling from it in strips.

I wanted to find Lisa. But not here. Not in this horrible place. It was the kind of place I'd read about and seen on TV a few times—someone would get hooked on drugs, drop out, and wind up living in a nasty apartment building like this.

Was that what happened to Lisa? Oh, God, I didn't want to know!

But I made myself keep going. I couldn't turn around now, even though I was terrified of what I might find.

Apartment 2A was at the end of the hall on the second floor. I stood outside the flaking, brown-painted door, took a deep breath, and knocked.

Footsteps sounded. A chain rattled. A bolt clicked, and the door creaked open.

Here we go. I stared at the old wooden floor, trying to prepare myself. *If Lisa's messed up, I'm bringing her home. Maybe on the South Central bus if I have to.*

"Can I help you?" a male voice asked.

When I glanced up, everything I'd been thinking flew out of my mind. All I could do was stare at the tall, dark-haired, incredibly gorgeous guy inside the door.

Chapter 14

Kerri

"I should eat," I said to Matt as we sat in the hotel restaurant on Saturday morning. It was a little before nine. Matt was scarfing down toast and eggs. I was staring at an English muffin. "I'll need plenty of energy for the photo shoot."

"An excellent idea," he said. He spread some grape jelly on a muffin half and handed it to me. "You're really nervous, aren't you?"

"Ha. It's an hour to the photo shoot, and butterflies are flapping around in my stomach. Big ones."

"You'll be great," he said, picking up his orange juice.

I nibbled a tiny bite of muffin. The butterflies didn't revolt, so I ate some more.

"I'm extremely nervous," I admitted. "But it's not a bad kind of nervous. It's like I'm so ready to prove myself, I can hardly wait."

Matt reached across the table and squeezed my hand. "You'll do great," he repeated.

It was the second time he'd said that. And he didn't sound very convincing. "Is something the matter?" I asked.

He shook his head. "It's just that we only have a few more hours left of the senior trip. I wish we could spend the morning together, since it's our last one here. But that's okay," he added. "I know how much modeling means to you. I'm really glad you have this chance."

"I wish we could be together the rest of the morning too," I agreed. "If Donna just hadn't ruined the contest, I'd already be signed with an agency. And we could have some time by ourselves today."

"Yeah." Matt frowned and pushed his plate aside.

Good going, Kerri, I said silently. *Mention Donna. That'll make the last day perfect.*

Still, Matt and I hadn't really discussed her since the first time she'd called. And I hadn't told him about last night's message yet.

I guess he should know, I thought. *He's involved in this as much as I was.*

"She called me yesterday," I said.

Matt's head snapped up. "Donna?"

I nodded. "She left me a message on the phone. She wants me to meet her this morning at the Starbucks across the street. I'm . . ."

"No way!" Matt interrupted, his eyes flashing. "You don't know Donna, Kerri. Believe me, if you give her the tiniest bit of encouragement, she'll blow it totally out of proportion. You can't go to meet her."

Whoa, I thought. *He's really freaking out.* "I'm not going to meet her," I told him quietly. "That's what I was going to say."

"Good." He reached for his orange juice. "Good." He said again. But this time it didn't sound as if he was saying it to me. He sounded almost as though he was saying it to himself.

I set the half-eaten muffin on my plate. The butterflies were quiet, but bells were suddenly going off in my head—alarm bells.

Something wasn't right. It seemed as though Matt knew Donna pretty well. Much better than he told me he did.

What was up with that?

Jessica

"Hi." The dark-haired guy glanced back and forth between Alex and me. "You two look a little confused," he said with a grin.

He was definitely right about that. I was confused and totally amazed. This guy was hot. Like a model or a movie star. Who was he, and what was he doing in this dump?

"Maybe you have the wrong apartment," he suggested. "This is 2A."

"It's the right apartment," I said. "But I must have gotten the address wrong or something." I was almost sure I hadn't, but what other explanation could there be? "I was looking for Lisa Carvelli. I thought she lived here."

He smiled at me, and a dimple appeared on the left side of his cheek. "You thought right."

"I did?" I said. "You know Lisa?"

"I sure do." He grinned again and pulled the door open wider. "Come on in. Lisa's in the living-room-slash-bedroom."

I was still so surprised, I couldn't move for a second. Then I felt Alex's hand close around mine. "Come on, Jess," he whispered. "Let's find out what's going on."

Right. That's what I'm here for, I reminded myself.

The door opened into a kitchen with barely enough space for one person to move around in. Everything in it was old and used. The cabinets had been painted dark brown, and the floor was covered with gray-speckled linoleum. Pretty ugly, but at least it was clean.

A theater poster for a play called *The Homecoming* was taped to the refrigerator door. The refrigerator was so old, it looked like it belonged in a museum.

Alex and I followed the guy single file through the kitchen, past a bathroom with black-and-pink tiles, and into the living-room-slash-bedroom.

It wasn't gigantic, but after the kitchen it seemed huge, with a high ceiling and two tall windows at one end.

I glanced around quickly. Scratched wooden floor, brick-and-board bookcase, more theater posters, a couple of plants. For furniture, there were a big chest of drawers, two chairs, and a round metal table.

Lisa was reading something, curled up at one end of a sagging, overstuffed couch.

Couch-slash-bed, probably.

"You've got some company, Lisa," the guy said, leaning against the kitchen doorway.

Lisa glanced up and dropped what she was reading. "Jessica! Alex?"

Alex said hi. I just stared at her. She was still kind of thin, but she looked better. Much better.

Shiny hair, clear skin, sparkling eyes. She couldn't look that good if she was on drugs, could she?

But she might if she was pregnant. *Oh, God.*

"How did you find me?" Lisa asked.

"I went to . . ." I started to say. Then I stopped. What difference did it make how I found her? "That doesn't matter," I told her. "You're the one who should be doing the explaining, Lisa. I'm your sister. I think I deserve to know what's going on."

"Oh, so *you're* Jessica," the guy said. "Lisa's told me a lot about you."

"Jess, this is Jacob," Lisa said. "Jacob, this is Jess. And a friend of hers, Alex."

Jacob and Alex shook hands. I managed to smile. Handshakes and polite introductions—this was unreal.

Jacob's dimple appeared as he flashed another smile. "Anybody want anything to drink? I think there's some orange juice. Or how about coffee?"

"I'd love some more coffee," Lisa told him. "Thanks."

"No problem." He disappeared into the kitchen. After a moment, we heard a loud rattling noise.

"Coffee beans," Lisa explained. "We like to grind them fresh."

"*We?*" I asked. "Who is he, your roommate?

Boyfriend? Husband? The father of your child?"

"Jessica!" Lisa looked shocked. "What are you talking about?"

"I don't know, Lisa. I don't know anything!" I cried. "That's why I'm here, to find out!"

"You're right. You deserve an explanation," Lisa admitted. She patted the couch. "Come on and sit down, and I'll tell you everything."

Finally, I thought.

I sat on the couch with Lisa. Alex took one of the chairs. The smell of coffee wafted in from the kitchen, but Jacob didn't return. I guess he was trying to give us some privacy.

"All right, here's what happened." Lisa drew in a deep breath. "I met Jacob at Marquette. I was taking an acting class—just for fun—and he was in it too." She paused, and a little smile played around her lips. "Jacob's my boyfriend, by the way. We're in love, Jessica. But I'm definitely not pregnant. Or married."

"Okay." Thank goodness.

"Anyway, major surprise—I found out I was really good at acting," Lisa continued. "I started to get serious about it. And Jacob—well, he's always been serious about it. He's been doing summer theater for five years. During a break, he auditioned for a production of *The Homecoming* here in

Chicago. And he got a part."

"Fine, but what about you?" I asked. I was starting to get impatient. I wanted to know about Lisa, not Jacob.

"I'm getting to that," Lisa said. "Jacob had to move here for the play, and we didn't want to be apart. So I came with him."

Just like that, I wanted to say. *You drop out of school, pack up and move to Chicago, all because of a guy*. But I didn't.

Lisa glanced around the room. "A friend of Jacob's sublet this place to him for a year. That's how long I've decided to stay here. Then I'm going back to Marquette."

"Really?" Alex asked.

"Oh, yeah. I definitely want a degree," Lisa told him.

"That's probably a good idea," he said.

"Yeah, but I still can't believe you actually quit," I told her. And I couldn't. I couldn't imagine myself doing something so radical.

"Well, I meant it when I said I've gotten serious about acting," Lisa told me. "I've gone on about twenty auditions already."

"And I guess you're working too," I said, thinking of Bliss and Fashion Statement.

"Oh, sure. We both work a couple of jobs," Lisa

replied. "It's tricky, though. Sometimes I have to call in sick or show up late because an audition comes up. Well, you saw what happened the other day. Rent is kind of expensive, so we stay here." She gestured around the room with her arm. "It isn't exactly a palace, but it's ours."

"Why didn't you tell me all this when I first saw you? Or call me?" I demanded. I couldn't hold it in any longer. She seemed happy, and she wasn't on drugs or pregnant. I should have been relieved, and I was. But I was also angry. "That was so unfair," I said. "I mean, you got me really, really worried! I was afraid you were doing drugs or something. Alex thought so too."

"That's ridiculous," Lisa said. "You know me, Jess. You know I don't do drugs."

"I *used* to know you," I told her. "That was before I saw you in Chicago, where you're not supposed to be, with your hair a mess and circles under your eyes. You wouldn't tell me what was going on, and you ran away from me. What's so ridiculous about thinking you were on drugs?"

Lisa lowered her eyes. "I see your point, Jess."

"I mean, I'm really glad you're okay, but Lisa, why did you have to scare me like that?" I asked.

"I'm sorry, Jess." Lisa sighed. "But you're so responsible. I was embarrassed to tell you I'd changed my whole life for a guy and a career that's tough to break into, to say the least. I knew you'd think I was totally out of my mind."

I winced. That was exactly what I was thinking.

"But you don't have to worry," she went on. "I'm not in any trouble. Besides, I didn't want you to get stuck between me and Mom and Dad. It's only for a year. And I thought if you didn't know what was going on, you wouldn't have to lie to them."

I'd almost forgotten about our parents. Now that she reminded me, I got even angrier. She just made my life more complicated than ever.

"God, Lisa." I jumped up from the couch. "Now I know, so I really am stuck! What am I supposed to do about that? Only for a year? Do you really think you can keep this a secret for that long? And what happens when Mom and Dad start asking me questions? What am I supposed to tell them?"

Before Lisa could reply, the phone rang.

Lisa froze. She stared at the phone as if it were a ticking bomb.

Jacob popped out of the kitchen and plucked the phone from the big chest of drawers. "Hello? Yes. Hi, Ms. Farber."

Lisa gasped and watched him intently.

"Wait . . . no, I'll get . . . but . . ." Jacob said. He

clutched the receiver tightly, looking very nervous. "I'm listening . . ."

Lisa kept watching him. Her eyes were wide, and she looked frightened, and I could tell she was holding her breath.

I suddenly realized I was holding my breath too. What if Lisa had been lying to me? She looked so scared. What if she really was in some kind of trouble?

I stared at Jacob, was still listening, nodding his head. "Don't worry. She will. She will, I promise."

I glanced at Alex. He shrugged and frowned. Neither one of us had a clue what was going on.

But it was obviously something serious.

I just hoped it wasn't as bad as it seemed.

Chapter 15

"Yes, okay," Jacob said into the phone. "I understand."

Lisa's face sort of sagged, like she knew exactly what he'd just been told.

God, what was it? It couldn't be good, not with that expression on Lisa's face. I'd started breathing again, but my heart was pounding, and my hands were actually shaking.

"Yes. I'll tell her right now," Jacob said. "Thanks, Ms. Farber."

Jacob hung up. For a split second, he didn't move. No one did.

I was holding my breath again, afraid to even imagine what had happened.

Then Jacob suddenly tore across the room, pulled Lisa from the couch, and swept her off her feet into a huge bear hug. "You got it!" he shouted at the top of his lungs.

Lisa gasped again. "I got it?"

"You got it!" Jacob repeated, spinning her around and around.

Alex and I looked at each other again. We didn't get it.

But it was easy to tell it was great news. I felt myself grinning even though I didn't know what about.

"You're not kidding, right?" Lisa laughed ecstatically.

"I wouldn't kid about something like that," Jacob told her, still spinning. "Ms. Farber was in a big hurry, that's why she asked me to give you the message."

Jacob stopped spinning and set Lisa on her feet. He pulled her close and gave her a big kiss. When they broke apart, they gazed at each other with shining eyes.

Jacob kissed Lisa's forehead, and pulled her close again, whispering something into her hair. They swayed back and forth, holding each other tightly. I could see Lisa's face—so bright and happy. So in love.

They're not just happy with the news, I thought. *They're happy with each other*. There was a major connection between them. I could feel it across the room.

"Okay, okay, wait; we're embarrassing Jess and Alex," Lisa said, pulling away from Jacob.

"No, you're not," I told her. "But I would kind of like to know what happened."

Lisa laughed and flopped onto the couch. "Barbara Farber is my agent," she said. "I auditioned for a play last week, and she just called to tell me I got a part."

"Lisa, that's great!" I said. In spite of everything, I really meant it. It was impossible *not* to be glad for her. "What play? Is it a big part?" I asked her.

"It's called *Inherit the Wind*, and I only have about four lines. And I'm in a couple of crowd scenes," she said.

"Hey, it's a great start," Jacob told her. He leaned down and kissed her again, then headed for the kitchen. "I'll get the coffee."

Lisa smiled as she watched him go. Then she looked at me. "Time to come back down to earth, I guess."

I felt like a real spoilsport, but I couldn't leave Chicago without getting some things straight with her. "Lisa, I'm really glad for you. And Jacob seems great. But what about Mom and Dad?" I asked. "When are you going to let them in on all this?"

Lisa shook her head. "I just don't know how to

tell them yet. They'll flip out. I know it."

Unfortunately, she was right. Both my parents were big on us studying hard, getting top grades, and going to college for at least four years. A scholarship to graduate school would be even better.

They'd never understand dropping out of college for a year to act, not to mention living with a guy.

I didn't exactly understand it, either. And I knew I should tell my parents. They'd freak, but it wouldn't last forever. They couldn't force Lisa to go to college. To live the kind of life they wanted her to live.

That's because it's her life, I realized. *Not Mom and Dad's. Not mine. Hers. And Lisa's got to make the choices. She's also got to live with the repercussions—good or bad.*

"Jess, I know I have to talk to Mom and Dad, and I'm going to," Lisa said. "But could you just not say anything yet? Let me figure out how to tell them in my own way."

Lisa was so happy. I really didn't want to ruin things for her. "I'll try to keep them in the dark, but only for a few weeks, Lisa," I said. "I won't lie to them forever. You have to figure out a way to tell them the truth. Soon."

"I will. I promise." Lisa reached over and hugged me. "Thank you, Jess."

Kerri

About half an hour before my photo shoot, I stepped into my black pants and pulled on a plain white shirt. My fingers shook as I buttoned it.

"What about jewelry?" Maya asked. She and Erin were helping me get everything together.

"The photographer might have some," I said. "But I guess I could take a couple of necklaces. How about the silver chain and the one with the little red hearts?"

Maya found them on the dresser and put them into a little cloth pouch. She stuck the pouch into my shoulder bag.

"Makeup?" Erin asked. "I brought some of mine, just in case you wanted to borrow it." She held up her fuzzy green makeup bag.

"Definitely. No black lipstick, though," I warned. "I don't want to look like a Goth."

"Goths are people too." Erin grinned. "Don't worry, Kerri, I won't slip any weird colors in." She gathered some lipstick and blush and eye shadow and put it in my makeup bag.

I started brushing my hair. The butterflies were

back in my stomach, performing all kinds of daredevil stunts.

But the warning bell about Matt was quiet now. It was going to stay that way too. No more doubting him. He didn't have to know Donna all that well to realize she was a nutcase. She'd stalked me and threatened me, after all.

Matt was my boyfriend. I knew him. He wasn't keeping any deep, dark secrets from me. He'd just been upset and mad when I told him that Donna had called again.

Donna was the one who should set off all my alarms. I couldn't pay attention to anything she said. She was just trying to confuse me.

"It's twenty after nine, Kerri," Maya said. "You'd better leave now."

"Definitely." I finished with my hair and stuck the brush into my bag. My heart was pounding already. "Do I have everything?"

"Makeup, jewelry, brush, hair clips, elastics—check," Erin said, poking around in the bag. "Wallet, directions, money, tissues—check." She zipped the bag and handed it to me.

I pressed a hand to my stomach. "Oh, boy."

"If you're going to throw up, do it now," Erin said. "There aren't any sick-sacks in your bag."

I managed to laugh. "I'll be okay."

Erin hugged me. "Good luck, Kerri. You're going to be fantastic. I wish I could come watch."

Maya was going to the shoot with me, but Erin had to stay behind and baby-sit Ms. Gomes. Jess had left earlier, and she still wasn't back.

"I wish Jess would at least call," Erin said. "I'm starting to get a little freaked."

I was a little worried too, but I had to force the whole Jess-Lisa thing out of my mind for the moment. I needed to stay focused for the photo shoot.

Erin walked us to the door. She'd decided to hide out in our room for a while so she wouldn't have to answer any questions about Jessica's whereabouts.

Erin gave me a thumbs-up and hugged me again, then Maya and I rode the elevator down to the lobby. We decided to take a taxi. No taking chances on the train this time.

"Whoa, there's a ton of people out there." Maya pointed toward the front doors. At least a dozen people stood in front of the hotel, looking up and down the street. "Let's hope they're not all trying to get cabs."

Maya hurried across the lobby. I followed behind her. I was looking toward the revolving door, worrying about getting a cab, when someone suddenly stepped in front of me.

Donna.

I stopped, but only for a split second. I didn't have time for this. Not now, not ever.

I started to go around her, but she stepped in my way again. Maya was already out the door. I made a move to follow her.

Donna reached out and grabbed my arm. "Stop. I think you'll want to hear what I have to say."

"Let go of me, Donna," I said through my teeth. I guess I should have been scared, and I was, a little. But mostly I was angry. I would not let her ruin anything again. "Let go," I repeated.

She did, and I stepped around her again and started walking toward the door.

"Well, if you don't want to know that your so-called boyfriend is sleeping with me, then I guess I won't tell you," she said.

That stopped me. I slowly turned around and walked back to her. "What did you say?"

"You heard me. Matt's been sleeping with me," she repeated. She shook her brown hair back and looked me in the eyes. "We've been seeing each other for a long time. And every time he has a fight with you, he runs to me."

"No," I told her. "You're lying. Or fantasizing.

You still want Matt back."

"Hel-lo? Are you listening?" she asked. "I still have Matt—part of the time, anyway."

"Shut up. You're a freak. Matt doesn't want anything to do with you. God, what am I doing, listening to this?" I said, turning to go.

"Remember the big fight you two had at the Cellar a couple of months ago?" Donna asked quickly. "After he left you that night, he came to me."

"You wish," I said. But how did she know about the fight?

Get a clue, Kerri, I told myself. *She's been lurking around for months. She was probably in the Cellar that night. Or she heard about it from kids she knows at South Central.*

I hated even remembering that fight. I had all these plans about how to keep our relationship going after we went off to different colleges. Matt started feeling trapped and accused me of trying to run his life.

"He was having a really rough time then," Donna went on. "His parents were pushing him to go to Purdue, remember? I wouldn't know that if he hadn't told me, right? Or about the fight either."

"Wrong," I said. "You know plenty of people who could have told you."

"Maybe. But I heard it from Matt," she said. "He was really upset. That schedule you made up freaked him out. And then you kissed somebody else right in front of him. So he came to me, like he always does. And we did way more than kiss."

"I am *not* listening to this." I started to walk away again.

"I'm not stupid. I know he cheats on me, Kerri," Donna called out. "I let him. But he's cheating on you too. And you don't even know it."

"Stop it!" I said furiously. "You're pathetic, you know? That's the only reason I haven't called the police. But the next time you come near me, that'll be the first thing I do."

I whirled around and ran for the door. I couldn't wait to get away from her. *Don't let her get to you,* I lectured myself. *Donna is crazy. You know she is.*

Matt is not sleeping with her. Everything she says to you is a lie.

It has to be.

Chapter 16

Jessica

"**W**hoa, it's almost ten-thirty," I said to Alex as we sat in the El train on the way back to the hotel. "I can't believe we're going home soon. And poor Erin—she must be crazy by now trying to avoid Ms. Gomes. I hope everything's okay. I'm really going to owe her after this."

"Mmm."

Alex was kind of quiet, and I remembered that he hadn't gotten much sleep.

"Thanks for coming with me," I told him. "It really helped having you there."

He smiled. "No problem."

"I am so relieved that Lisa's okay." I sighed, settling back in the seat. "I was imagining the absolute worst, and it turned out I was worried over nothing. Well, not exactly nothing," I added. "My parents are going to be furious when they find out about her."

"Yeah, well, they should be," Alex declared. "I can't believe what Lisa's doing. It's so . . . so . . ." He shook his head. "I mean, she's ruining her life."

I stared at him in surprise. How could he think that? Hadn't he seen how happy Lisa was? How much in love she and Jacob were? "Do you really think so?" I asked.

He stared back at me, just as surprised. "Don't you?"

I knew Alex expected me to agree with him, but I couldn't. Which was strange, because we usually agreed on most things—we liked pepperoni pizza and marshmallows in cocoa and almost never turned homework in late because it just caused more stress.

"Come on, Jess, dropping out of college to be an *actress?*" Alex asked skeptically. "I mean, give me a break."

I didn't like the condescending tone in his voice. "Well, but it's only for a year," I reminded him. "Then she's going back to school. She said so, remember?"

"Sure, that's what she says *now*," he argued. "But she just got a part in a play. Maybe she'll get lucky and get another part or two this year."

"What's wrong with that?"

"She might decide to forget about college for

good," Alex pointed out. "But then what if the acting jobs dry up? She'll be right back waiting tables or whatever and living in a dump."

"I guess that could happen," I admitted. "I don't exactly agree with what she's doing either. But it's her life, isn't it?"

It felt weird to be arguing about this with Alex. Because there was a time I would have totally agreed with him. But I'd changed, I realized. I wasn't sure when it happened. Or why.

I just knew I didn't see things the same way I used to. The way Alex did now.

"Sure, it's Lisa's life," Alex said. "She's just messing it up, that's all. She's doing everything the wrong way."

I thought about that as the train rumbled along. Before this trip, I would have agreed with that too—there was a right way and a wrong way to get what you wanted. Like I wanted to be a writer, and I thought the only way to do it was to go to NYU.

But things could change. I didn't expect them to, but still, I couldn't box myself in. If an opportunity came up that didn't follow my plan, I had to at least consider taking it. That's what Lisa had done. And I really hoped it worked out for her.

"Sometimes you have to take chances to get

what you want," I said to Alex. "Look at me—I took some major ones to find Lisa. And it worked. I mean, I was so worried about her, and now I know she's okay. That would have never happened if I chose to just sit in my room. I'd probably still be worried about her."

"That's different," he said. "You'd never drop out of college to do something like Lisa did, would you?"

I didn't answer right away. I tried to picture myself doing it. But it was hard because nothing had come up to make me want to change my life so radically. "No," I said doubtfully. "But—"

"I didn't think so." Alex slung his arm around my shoulders and pulled me against him. "That's why I'm glad I'm going out with the practical sister."

Going out? Is that what we were doing? I sneaked a glance at Alex. He looked cheerful. Sort of content. He obviously thought we were going out. That we were back together again.

But when did we decide that?

Kerri

Instead of arriving at the studio feeling sure of myself and ready to wow everybody with my modeling, I felt furious and ready to cry.

"I should have kept on going," I muttered to Maya as Tom, the photographer, made some adjustments to his camera. His studio was in a big loft, with white walls and tracks of lights that were hanging from the ceiling. A plain paper backdrop ran down one wall onto the floor. That was where the models would pose. The room also had makeup mirrors and a curtained changing area.

Maya and I sat with two other girls on some plastic chairs in front of the mirrors. "Why did I stop and listen to her?" I asked. "How could I be so totally stupid?"

"You have to push it out of your mind, Kerri. She just said those things to hurt you. Matt doesn't want her and she doesn't want you to have Matt. I bet she's hoping you'll believe everything she says and dump him." Maya handed me my brush. "Here. Your hair's all tangled."

"Not as tangled as my brain," I said, dragging the brush through my hair. "Donna's timing is perfect. The modeling contest, now the photo shoot. I can't believe I let her turn me into a total wreck again. Ha. Actually, I can believe it. I mean, what else is new?"

"Kerri? I'm ready for you," Tom called out.

"Oh, God," I murmured.

Maya took my brush back and gave me an encouraging smile. "Go on. You'll be great."

I pulled in a deep breath and walked across the room. While I stood in front of the backdrop, Tom quickly took some readings with his light meter. He was about thirty, with sharp blue eyes and a no-nonsense attitude.

"Okay, let's have some tunes and we'll get started," he said.

He turned on a CD player, filling the loft with the music of Third Eye Blind. One of Matt's favorite bands.

Don't think about Matt, I ordered myself.

But Matt was all I *could* think about. Matt . . . and Donna.

That schedule you made freaked him out, Donna had said. *And then you kissed someone else right in front of him.*

I'd heard her say it at the hotel, and I was so angry I'd brushed it off. But now the words were practically shouting in my head, louder than the music in the studio.

"Kerri, you want to move to the music a little?" Tom called out.

I started to move, but I felt like a robot. The clicking, whirring sounds of the camera faded away, and Donna's words filled my head again.

That schedule you made. . . You kissed someone in front of him.

I did make a schedule. When I was trying to work out a long-distance relationship with Matt, I actually sat down and charted a schedule for phone calls and weekend visits.

And when he got mad about it, I thought he wanted to see other people. I thought if he saw me kiss another guy on the cheek he'd change his mind. But then the guy turned his head and planted one on my lips.

Then Matt really got mad.

Donna might have heard about our fight from somebody else. But only one person could have told her the details.

Matt.

"Head up, Kerri," Tom instructed. "Look at the camera. You're not connecting."

I lifted my chin and followed the camera with my eyes as Tom moved around in front of me. I tried to connect.

But I started to think of other arguments between Matt and me. The way he would be incommunicado for hours or days afterward. Like the time I got the day wrong and wasn't home when he came by to pick me up for a date. Like the time he got angry because all I talked about was modeling. I accused him of not caring about what I wanted. He denied it and stormed off. And avoided me for two days.

Now I knew where he'd been. Not holed up in his room, sulking. Not driving around, thinking things through.

No. He'd been with Donna. Letting her make him feel better.

Why hadn't I seen it?

Tears suddenly stung my eyes. I shook my head and blinked furiously. I would not cry. Not here. Not now.

But the stinging got stronger, and suddenly everything grew blurry. I tried to stop the tears, but I couldn't.

"Okay, hold it a sec," Tom said. He walked up to me and leaned close so I could hear him over the music. "This isn't going too well. I guess you know that."

I swiped some tears from my cheeks and nodded.

"Maybe we should postpone your test shoot," he suggested. "I've got other girls waiting, and I'm working on a tight schedule. You can come back and try again when you're ready."

"Just . . ." I swallowed the lump in my throat. "Just give me half a minute. Please? Half a minute."

I hurried over to Maya. "Kerri, what's wrong?" she asked. "I thought I was imagining it, but you really are crying."

"I know." I ignored the curious stares of the other two girls and tried to ignore Tom, who was actually checking his watch. "I was thinking of Matt and Donna, and I just lost it. Tom wants me to quit for today. I don't blame him."

"You can't quit." Maya grabbed my bag and pulled out a wad of tissues. "After all you've done to get here, you'd actually let Donna ruin it for you? I can't believe you're going to let her turn you into a loser!"

Maya stuffed the tissues into my hand and glared at me. She looked furious, and it really gave me a jolt. Maya's usually kind of quiet. She's a really kind, sympathetic person. Now she was actually being harsh. Calling me a loser.

Well, Kerri, you might as well admit it, I thought. Maya was right. Donna and Matt couldn't ruin this for me—I had to let them. And if I did, I really was a loser.

I wanted this too much to let that happen. I wasn't about to blow it twice. There was no third chance.

I wiped my eyes and cheeks. Maya handed me a compact, some eyeshadow and blush, and I quickly repaired my makeup. "Okay?" I asked.

"It's perfect," Maya declared. "Now go be a model."

I hurried back across the room. "Thanks for waiting," I said to Tom. "I'm ready now."

He nodded and picked up his camera. The music was still playing, and this time I listened to it, not to any of Donna's words.

"Look over here, Kerri," Tom called out. "Give me a smile . . . great! Fantastic!"

The camera clicked and whirred, and I kept smiling.

Chapter 17

Jessica

"I can't believe I brought this much stuff to Chicago," I declared, tossing an armload of clothes on my bed. "I'm definitely traveling lighter next time."

"What next time?" Alex asked me. He was stretched out on Erin's bed in my hotel room. He'd already packed, so he'd decided to hang out with me while I tried to fit everything back into my bags for the trip home.

"There won't be a next time," he reminded me. "I just realized—this is our last school trip."

"Oh, no—you're right!" That made me a little sad, and I decided not to dwell on it just then. I was feeling too good—Lisa was all right, and I'd made it back to the hotel without getting caught.

Of course, I'd still have detention when we got home. But that was nothing compared to what could have happened.

"I guess it is the last major trip," I agreed. "But the class will still do things together—the spring picnic, Senior Breakfast, Senior Prank Day . . ."

"The prom," Alex added. "Now *that's* going to be a trip. The limo companies are going to clean up."

I laughed, and stuffed some socks into my duffel bag. "We don't have to take a limo, you know."

Wait. Had I just said "we"?

"Are you kidding?" Alex asked. "A limousine is practically required."

I smiled, but I was still thinking about what I'd said before. *We don't have to take a limo.*

Funny. On the train, Alex talked like we were a couple again. Now I was doing it too. I still didn't know how it happened. And I didn't know if I wanted it to happen.

Alex held up the rolled-up sketch he'd bought for me at Navy Pier. "Don't forget to take this."

"Definitely not. It'll always remind me of the day we ditched Ms. Gomes." I laughed, and held out my hand for the sketch.

Alex stretched out his arm. But instead of letting go of the sketch, he grabbed my wrist with his other hand and pulled me onto Erin's bed.

His arms came around me. Our lips were almost touching. "It'll always remind me of the carousel," he said, and he kissed me. "Remember?"

I nodded.

"You wanted to get rid of Ms. Gomes," Alex said. "I didn't care about that. All I wanted to do was this." He kissed me again, more deeply. His hands slid up my back.

I waited for that familiar flutter in my stomach, but it didn't come. Something was wrong. Or missing. It just didn't feel right. I wasn't sure why.

This used to be all I wanted, I thought. *Being with Alex, having him for a boyfriend, knowing he'd always be there. But now . . .*

The door burst open. "Okay, we . . . oops!" Erin cried.

I quickly rolled off Alex and sat up.

Erin staggered into the room, loaded down with duffel bags. Glen was right behind her, carrying more bags and a couple of backpacks.

"What's all that?" I asked, pushing my hair out of my face. My very red face.

Erin just grinned at me.

Glen was smiling too, but at least he answered. "Maya's and Kerri's stuff. We packed for them in case they didn't get back from the photo shoot in time."

"They'd better hurry," Alex said. "The buses are leaving in about forty minutes." He squeezed my hand and stood up.

I scooted off the bed and started packing my own stuff again.

"Hey, what's this?" Glen asked, picking up a fuzzy bag from the dresser top.

"It's my makeup bag," Erin told him.

Glen turned it around in his hands. "Looks like a hedgehog. Or a fuzzy football. Hey, Alex, go long!"

Glen tossed the makeup back toward Alex. Alex raced toward the door and caught it, then passed it back to Glen.

Erin crossed over to me. "Sorry for barging in on you like that," she whispered. "So, are you guys really back together? I guess he's got to break up with Suzanne when he gets home."

I glanced over my shoulder. Glen and Alex were still tossing the bag back and forth.

"Hey, you guys, be careful with that!" Erin called out. She turned back to me. "This is so great," she whispered. "I know you thought you were over him, but I guess true love never dies, huh?"

I didn't know what to say. True love? Was that what Alex and I had?

"It's perfect—we've all got boyfriends now," Erin said. "Finally all our social lives are easy."

The makeup bag flew through the air. Erin

reached out and snagged it before it crashed against the door.

"Interception!" Glen cried. He raced toward Erin, trying to snatch the bag back.

Alex flopped down on my bed. "It won't be long now, and we'll be on our way back to good old Madison," he said. "Let's get together on Sunday, okay? I've already got it planned out."

That didn't surprise me. Alex was very big on planning. So was I. But maybe not as much as before. "What?" I asked.

"Three things." He held up his fingers and ticked them off. "We go to the mall—a new Creed CD's coming out, and I want to get it. Then we go back to my house and hang out with Josh. But on the way back, we rent a video so we can watch it alone after Josh goes to bed."

Josh was Alex's totally adorable four-year-old nephew.

"I can't wait to see his face when you come in the door with me," Alex said. "He's missed you, you know."

"I've missed him too," I said. I'd hardly seen him since Alex and I broke up. It was so cute, the way he called me "Aunt Jessie."

It would be fun to see Josh and give him a big hug and play games with him. But going to the mall, getting a CD, renting a video with Alex? I wasn't sure about that.

Not that it would be horrible or anything. It would be nice. And very, very easy. I didn't even have to say a word. All I had to do was go along with it, and I'd become Alex's girlfriend again. We could fall into the same routine without missing a step.

The makeup bag came flying toward Alex. He caught it and jumped up, joining the game again.

He was smiling and happy.

No wonder. He had everything planned out, and that was the way he liked it. Which was fine— for him.

But it wasn't fine for me, I realized. Not anymore. After all, one reason I broke up with him was because our relationship was too planned. Too predictable. Face It too boring.

I thought of Lisa and Jacob. The looks on their faces when they smiled at each other. The love between them. The connection.

Alex and I just didn't have that connection. Not anymore. That's why kissing him didn't feel right. The chemistry was missing.

I wanted something else—somebody else, even though I didn't know who he was yet. But I definitely wanted the same kind of connection that

Lisa had to Jacob. I might not have a boyfriend for a while. I'd probably get lonely. But I'd have to take that chance.

Sometimes you have to take chances to get what you want. That's what I'd said to Alex on the train.

He didn't think like that. Maybe he couldn't think like that. But that was the problem.

I realized that I couldn't do it. I couldn't let myself get back together with him. It would be fun, for a while. It would definitely take care of the dating situation. Like Erin said, all our social lives would be easy.

But it would be all wrong.

I sighed and tucked a sweater into my duffel bag. I wasn't sure about everything I wanted. Actually I was more sure of what I didn't want.

And I didn't want Alex—even if it would be easy.

Maybe *because* it would be easy.

Chapter 18

Kerri

"**A**re you sure, Kerri?" Maya asked as we pushed through the hotel doors into the lobby. "Are you totally sure?"

It was about the tenth time she'd asked me since we left the photo shoot. I didn't blame her. I'd asked myself the same question at least a hundred times.

The answer was yes.

I had to break up with Matt.

Was he sleeping with Donna? That I wasn't sure about. But it didn't matter whether he'd slept with her or only kissed her or just held her hand.

He'd never quit seeing her. And he'd been lying to me about it for months.

"When are you going to tell him?" Maya asked.

"As soon as we get home," I replied. "I haven't figured out exactly what to say yet. The bus ride will give me time to think."

"Kerri, Maya—over here!" Erin shouted, and she waved her arms over her head. "We've got your stuff all ready!"

The lobby was crowded with all the South Central kids waiting for the buses. They sat on their bags or on the floor, talking and joking. Alex and Glen and Luke were tossing Erin's makeup bag around. Teachers circulated with clipboards, making sure everybody was there.

I did a quick survey. Didn't see Matt. Good. I wasn't ready to face him yet.

Maya and I made our way through the crowd toward a huge potted rubber plant near the elevators, where Erin and Jessica stood surrounded by duffel bags.

"What happened at the photo shoot?" Erin asked immediately.

Jess nodded eagerly. "We're dying to know."

I shrugged. The shoot seemed like a hundred years ago.

Jess frowned at me. I knew she could tell something was the matter.

"Kerri was fantastic," Maya said quickly. "There were two other girls there, and they were really impressed. So was the photographer."

"That's just great, Kerri," Jess said. She was still staring at me curiously, but she'd obviously figured out that I didn't want to talk about the shoot right then. "When will you hear from the modeling agency?"

"I'm not sure. Sometime next week, I guess." I glanced around the lobby. Still no sign of Matt.

Then the elevator opened, and there he was. Tall, incredible blue eyes, athletic body.

A slow smile spread across his face when he saw me.

I made myself smile back, but my face felt so stiff I thought it would crack.

"Hey, you're here," Matt said. He put his arm around me. "How did it go?"

"Fine," I managed to say.

Pause.

"Kerri was fantastic," Maya repeated, breaking the silence.

Matt squeezed my shoulders and kissed the top of my head.

I almost cringed. I felt like flinging his arm off. I was so furious and so hurt, I wanted to scream at him right there in the lobby in front of the whole senior class.

All of a sudden, I knew I couldn't wait until we got home. I had to talk to him now. I had to tell him it was over between us.

There was still time. The buses hadn't even

arrived yet. "Let's go sit down," I said to Matt. "I'll tell you everything."

I gave Maya a look that said, "Here goes."

Maya took the hint. "Come on, guys," she said to Erin and Jess. "Let's go buy some stuff to eat on the bus."

I walked around the potted plant and over to an empty overstuffed chair, but I didn't sit down. Matt came with me, dropped into the chair, and started to pull me onto his lap.

"Don't," I said, stepping away. "I don't want to sit. I want to talk."

"I'll let you talk, I promise." He grinned. "But I'd hear better if you sat on my lap."

Oh, God, this was going to be hard! He was so good-looking and sexy and funny.

And such a liar.

"Matt, please listen to me," I said. "I know about Donna, okay? I know you've been seeing her the whole time you and I have been going together."

That made the grin vanish. His face flushed, and he quickly stood up. "What are you talking about?"

"About the night we had that fight at the Cellar, for one thing," I told him. "Donna was waiting for me in the lobby today when I left for the photo shoot. She told me about that night—the night you ran to her and told her how I'd made up a schedule for seeing each other in college. How I'd kissed someone else to make you jealous. The night you slept with her."

Matt shoved his fists into his pockets. His face was dark red now. He didn't say it wasn't true. He didn't say anything.

"You're the only one who could have told her that stuff," I said. "What else did you tell her? Does she know every detail about us?"

"No!" he finally burst out. "I only told her about the schedule because . . ." He suddenly broke off.

I closed my eyes for a second. Now I really knew it was true. It hurt so much I felt like I couldn't breathe.

"Kerri," Matt said. "Please—"

"I can't believe how stupid I've been," I said. "I mean, when Donna started stalking me, you brushed it off. And when you couldn't do that anymore, you got really tense. You told me not to listen to her or believe a thing she said because she was nuts."

"She is," he muttered.

"Right," I snapped. "And not only did you lie to me about seeing her, you actually put me in danger. Didn't you care about that? Or did you think you could talk her out of stalking me?"

Matt didn't reply.

"All this time I thought you were so worried about me," I said. "But you were worried about her too—you were afraid she'd tell me what was really going on. Well, she finally did."

Matt took a deep breath. "I didn't mean for this to happen, Kerri," he murmured.

"What—that I'd find out?" I asked.

"No. That I'd keep seeing Donna," he said. "I don't know . . . I can't explain it. It just happened."

"And now it's over," I told him.

He nodded. "Definitely. I'll break it off with her the minute we get home."

I slowly shook my head. "That's not what I meant," I said. "I meant it's over between you and me."

Matt's face paled, then flushed all over again. "Kerri, no! I'll get rid of Donna," he promised.

He looked shocked and hurt and . . . lost.

Exactly how I felt.

I wanted to believe him so much. But how could I? I thought I knew him, and he'd been lying to me for months. I thought I loved him, but . . .

My chest ached, and my throat was so tight I could hardly say the words. "I'm sorry, Matt," I choked out. "But it really is over."

I walked away before he could say anything else. My eyes were filling up, and everything was blurry, but I managed to spot my friends standing in front of the hotel coffee shop.

By the time I reached them, the tears were dripping off my chin, and I was crying too hard to speak.

My friends gathered around and hugged me. "Maya told us about Matt," Jess murmured. "I'm so sorry."

"Me too," Erin said, patting my shoulder.

Maya handed me a bunch of tissues. "I know you feel awful. But it'll be okay, really."

Jess squeezed my hand. "Yeah. It will all work out. You did the right thing, breaking up with him."

I nodded, and buried my face in the tissues. If only the right thing didn't hurt so much.

Chapter 19

Jessica

The front door opened when I was halfway up the walkway to my house.

"Welcome home, Jessica!" Mom called out.

"Hi, Mom, thanks. Hi, Dad."

My father came onto the front porch and took one of my bags as I climbed the steps. "How was the trip back?"

"Oh, fine. Kind of boring." I followed him through the front door and dropped my duffel and backpack. "We all slept a lot."

Mom gave me a hug, then Dad did. I knew they were happy to see me, but I also knew it wouldn't be long before I got a lecture about the hotel room party. The line would be that I let them down and jeopardized my college career.

It wouldn't be pleasant, but I could take it.

But lying to them about Lisa was going to be tough. I was already feeling so guilty, it was hard to look them in the eyes.

On the trip back, I tried to come up with some kind of story. I decided to tell part of the truth—she had a new boyfriend, and she was in a play. So she was either rehearsing or out on a date. I would just leave out minor parts, like quitting school and moving to Chicago.

But I hadn't thought it through very carefully. I wasn't ready to test it. Maybe I could put it off for a while. "Whoa, I'm tired," I said, which was true. "I'm going to unpack and maybe take a nap."

"You'll never get to sleep tonight if you do that, Jessica," Mom said. "Besides, I want to hear about Chicago. Let Dad take your bags upstairs while we go into the kitchen. I made some brownies."

This was probably when I'd get the lecture, I decided. Maybe Lisa's name wouldn't even come up. While Dad hefted my bags, I followed Mom down the hall into the kitchen.

The old brown linoleum immediately reminded me of Lisa's apartment.

"Sit, Jessica," Mom said. She put a plate of brownies on the table. "I want to talk to you."

"Mom, I'm sorry about what happened in Chicago," I told her, pulling out a chair. "The party was—"

"We can discuss that later," Mom said, sitting

opposite me. "Right now I want to talk about Lisa."

I started feeling panicky. I wasn't ready yet. I'd never be able to pull it off!

"Two times this week I've tried to call your sister, and there's been no answer," Mom told me. "She hasn't called here, either. I just don't know what to think."

"Well . . ." I said slowly, trying to get my thoughts together. "I'm sure she's really busy. Maybe she has a big test coming up."

"Too busy to call home once in a while?" Mom asked. "So busy she's never in her room? Jessica, I'm worried. Has she called you? Do you have any idea where she is?"

Here goes, I thought. I'd promised Lisa I'd cover for her. I had to start now.

Kerri

Monday morning. Back to school. I was so not in the mood to go that I'd decided I'd fake being sick.

It wasn't hard, because I still felt awful about breaking up with Matt. I knew I had to do it, but I couldn't look on the bright side yet.

I ambled down the hall into the living room of our apartment, where my mother was shoving things into her big red totebag. She's a guidance counselor at one of the junior high schools.

"Kerri, aren't you dressed yet?" she asked. "It's—"

Before she could tell me how late I was, and before I could say I wasn't feeling well, the phone rang. She reached for it and accidentally knocked it off the coffee table.

"I'll get it," I told her, picking it up. "Hello?"

"Yes, Kerri Hopkins, please."

I recognized the voice right away. It was Rachel Santos!

I glanced at my mother, trying to cover the fact that I was freaking out with excitement. "It's for me," I mouthed. She pointed to my bathrobe, pointed to her watch, gave me a wave, and let herself out the door.

"This is Kerri," I said into the phone. "Ms. Santos?"

"That's right. Hi, Kerri. I've got your pictures back."

Everything seemed to freeze, even my heart. "You did?"

"Yes." Ms. Santos paused. I could hear paper shuffling. *My pictures*, I thought. *Is she admiring them or tossing them into the wastepaper basket?*

"Okay," she said briskly. "Here's the deal. The shots are actually pretty good."

Yes! My heart started beating again.

"I don't think you're ready for the Chicago agency yet, but . . ."

But what? I wondered.

"Hightower has an office in Madison," she said. "We'd like you to be part of that, for now anyway. You're good, but you need some experience, and our Madison office is sort of a stepping-stone."

My heart was racing now, and I felt a grin spread across my face.

A stepping-stone meant I was on my way up. I was going to be a model!

The apartment door suddenly flew open, and Mom bustled in. She grabbed the carton of juice she'd left on the coffee table and hurried back out.

"This is great news, Ms. Santos," I said as soon as the door closed. "I'd love to work for the Madison office!"

Ms. Santos gave me a name and phone number. I grabbed a pencil from the shelf under the coffee table and jotted them down on the back of a magazine.

"I've already told them about you," Ms. Santos said. "They'll be expecting you to call. Good luck, Kerri."

I hung up and sank down onto the couch, clutching the magazine to my chest. But I was too excited to sit still. I jumped up and began whirling around the living room, laughing out loud.

I'd made it. I was going to be a model. Wait until I told Jess. And Erin and Maya.

And Mom.

Oh. Right. I stopped spinning and sat back down on the couch. *Time to come back to earth,* I thought.

I *was* going to be a model.

But now I had to convince my mother to let me do it.

Here's a
sneak peek at
Seventeen's latest book,

THE TRUTH ABOUT
GIRLFRIENDS.

It's an all-you-need,
totally honest guide to making
and keeping the best friends ever.

Check it out!

8 chapter

Getting Friendly

FRIENDSHIP RULE:
True girlfriends like you for who
you are—so when you're making
new friends don't be afraid to
be yourself!

Maybe you've moved to a new town and don't know anyone. Or maybe you've switched schools and have to work your way into a new crowd. Or maybe you've lived in the same town your entire life, but this year all your close pals are off to private school, leaving you to navigate the hallways of your public school alone. Whatever the situation—**you're in need of some friendly faces**.

Don't panic. Making new friends is not as tough, or as scary, as it sounds. Don't believe us? Check out the info in this chapter.

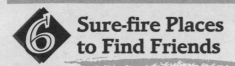

Sure-fire Places to Find Friends

Okay, so you have no friends. At least, none in the immediate vicinity. We admit it—a situation like this can make you want to curl up on your couch with a stack of your favorite movies and sulk. But—news flash!—you're not going to meet any potential friends in your living room! The only way to find new girlfriends is to **get out of the house** and meet new people. Come on—give it a shot. We've listed six great places to meet, mingle, and get to know below.

----

1. AFTER-SCHOOL ACTIVITIES. Think about what you like to do in your free time and find an activity that centers on that. Do you like to write? Join the school newspaper or yearbook staff. Are you a closet actor or shower singer? Try out for the school play or join the choir. You'll automatically have stuff in common with the people who are already members—which means you'll have a head start when you decide to get friendly!

2. THE LOCAL COFFEE SHOP/FOOD-RELATED HANGOUT. Ever notice how everyone flocks to the pizza joint, the ice cream parlor, the café, or the food court? It's because food is social. And if you're looking to make friends, social is good. Bring a book or magazine to glance at if you don't want to seem like you're weirdly scoping out the crowd. Or, if you're ultra-shy, think about getting a part-time job at one of these places. That way, you'll *have* to talk to people to get your job done— and maybe you'll meet some new girlfriends in the process.

3. HIGH SCHOOL VARSITY B-BALL AND FOOTBALL GAMES.

GO TEAM!

Does the whole town rally around the home team when they compete? Join in! And feel free to comment about the game to the varsity fan sitting next to you.

4. THE MUSIC STORE.

This is a prime spot to strike up a conversation. After all, who doesn't like to talk about their favorite bands? Jet over to the music store in town, or at the mall, and walk the aisles. If you spot a potential girlfriend shuffling through the Sarah McLaughlin CDs, and you're a huge fan yourself, head on over and start some music-related conversation.

5. VOLUNTEER GROUPS.

Check out what community service groups in your area are doing, and then sign yourself up. It's likely that there will be lots of people from your school doing the exact same thing. Think about the local animal shelter, senior citizen center, or soup kitchen. Not only will you be making friends, but by donating your time to these worthy causes, you'll be making a difference.

6. CHURCH OR SYNAGOGUE– or wherever your religion takes you. Almost every religious organization has a youth group. Part of the point of that group is to provide a place where teens with similar interests can get together and get to know each other. Amen to that!

RENT IT, SEE IT, LIVE IT:

Now and Then (1995/PG-13). Five unlikely friends (Demi Moore, Rosie O'Donnell, Rita Wilson, Julianne Moore, and Melanie Griffith) find themselves bonded to one another from childhood through the birth of their own children.

Breaking the Ice

Okay, so you've put yourself in situations where there are new people to meet. Now all you have to do is talk to them.

Granted, going up to a group of four girls alone can be an intimidating prospect. (Of course, if you feel bold enough to do it, go for it, girl.) But maybe you'd be more comfortable approaching a potential pal when she's by herself. Wait until she's standing at her locker, in the lunch line, or waiting around to talk to a teacher after class. Then move in.

So here you are . . . standing face-to-face with a potential girlfriend. You want to sound cool, but **what do you say?** Hey, you don't have to invent something ultrahip right on the spot! Cheat a little—we won't tell. Have a few icebreakers in your head before you open your mouth. (It sounds corny, but it works!) Check out the icebreakers below and choose your favorites!

Icebreaker #1: A compliment will get 'em every time.

Say you walked into Starbucks and spotted someone from your gym class. You stand next to her on line, but after your initial "hey" you're not sure what to say. That's when you notice the supercool skirt she's wearing. At this point, it's perfectly legit to say something like "Hey, I really love that skirt—where did you get it?"

It's bound to jump-start a conversation because she's

guaranteed to respond well to someone who's telling her her style is fab. Continue the chat by asking her where she likes to shop, whether she's ever gone to the monthly flea market, or the cool boutiques. If you two really connect, you might even end up with a shopping partner next weekend!

Icebreaker #2: Be honest.

Sometimes the simple approach is best. So if you're in an environment where you're feeling tongue-tied, admit it. Walk up to a friendly-looking person and say "Hi. I'm feeling kind of weird—I don't know anybody here."

Sure, you're playing the sympathy card—hoping the other person will take pity on you and hang with you. But the hard-core fact is—this works! Only the most heartless of strangers would ignore you in this situation. So go for it!

Maybe all this sounds like no prob to you. Or maybe you're sitting there thinking, "Are they nuts? No way am I going to go up to some strange girl and make conversation!" Well, we wouldn't make you look stupid. Ever. By opening yourself up to new places, experiences, and people, you'll find girlfriends who are right for you. Guaranteed.

Some people are naturally outgoing, and some need to work at meeting new people. What's your deal? Find out below.

Keep track of how many times you answer "A", "B", or "C" to get your score.

1 You see the new girl in school walking to class alone. You:

A. rush up to her and ask what she's doing Friday night.

B. grab your best friend and approach the new girl together, to see if she needs directions to the gym or anything.

C. smile and keep walking to your locker.

2 Your math teacher asks for volunteers to stand at the blackboard and demonstrate problem five from your homework assignment. You spent hours last night figuring that one out perfectly, so you:

A. immediately raise your hand and say "I'll do it!"

B. look around, and when you notice that no one else has raised their hand, offer to do it yourself.

C. sit there quietly, hoping you don't get called on.

3 At a party, you see your crush from social studies, standing alone in front of the snack table. You decide to:

A. go up to him and say "Hey, you're in my history class, right?"

B. slowly make your way to his side, then stand there for a few minutes before saying hi.

C. take a few minutes to mentally list the pros and cons of approaching him, then chicken out.

4 On your way home from school, a girl you vaguely recognize from biology stops to ask directions to Trina's Treasures, a local thrift shop. You don't know, so you:

A. spend ten minutes explaining that while you can't get her to Trina's Treasures, you *can* point her in the direction of Secondhand Rose, the coolest vintage shop within the county limits.

B. tell her you aren't sure how to get there, but that the gas station on the corner of Main and Chestnut has Chamber of Commerce maps.

C. smile and say you don't know, sorry.

5 After school you scoop ice cream at Fred and Ethel's in town. When a group of kids from your school comes in wearing face paint in the school colors, you say:

A. "Hey, you guys came from the pep rally, right? I've been dying to know—was the mascot's act as funny as it was last year?"

B. "How's it going? Did you just come from the pep rally?"

C. "Hi, do you guys know what you want?"

Scoring

Mostly A's—Way out there

There's no way you'll ever be caught without friends for very long. You take advantage of a solo situation (like being stuck at a party by yourself) and turn it into a meet-and-greet opportunity. It's cool that you are outgoing and chatty, but remember not to overwhelm potential pals (who might be a bit more shy) with your superfriendly ways.

Mostly B's—Out and about

You know when to swallow your nervousness and be social, but you do have a quiet, shy side to you as well, which makes for a great balance! While you may not launch right into a friendly conversation with a total stranger, you are probably really good at sending out friendly vibes, which hint at your social nature.

Mostly C's—In your shell

Yeah, we know. It can be really hard to open up and talk to people, especially when you have to make the first move, but you can do it! Just ease into it. Start by talking to acquaintances in class or at an after-school club, and then work yourself up to the bolder stuff, like showing up at a party by yourself. The more you do it, the easier it gets. We promise.

Common (and Uncommon!) Denominators

Meeting new people is only the first step in building friend-ships. Next you have to figure out which people you'd really like to get to know.

See, new girlfriends are kind of like boyfriends: You strike up a relationship because you are immediately attracted to something about that person—whether it's her remarkable confidence, her easy-going nature, her sense of humor, or her cool insights on one of your shared interests.

But while common interests may spark a friendship, don't freak out if, somewhere along the way, you realize that your new pal isn't the spitting image of yourself. Once you get beyond your shared enthusiasm for the newest boy band, you may discover that you and your friend are pretty different.

That's okay! Because a **terrific friendship is also about learning from the other person.**

Say you'd never even considered going to a James Bond flick, but your pal is an expert on all things 007. Why not check out a couple of old movies with her? Even if you don't become a card-carrying member of the Bond Fan Club, you are opening yourself up to new experiences, and seeing things from your friend's perspective.

Then, the next time she suggests a movie marathon, you can fill her in on the fact that Cameron Crowe was making amazing films long before *Jerry Maguire* and *Almost Famous* ever hit the big screen. Invite her over to watch *Say Anything*. Add popcorn, and watch the friendship blossom.

Friendship Builders

I t may sound cheesy, but one of the coolest parts of a new friendship is the intense, getting-to-know-you conversations you'll have. If you're in a silly mood, there are tons of fun games you can play to get to know each other better.

1. TOP FIVE MOVIES OF ALL TIME. Go ahead, list yours first. Then tell your new friend why you chose those movies. Reverse the process and learn something cool about your new bud.

MY FAVORITES:
1.
2.
3.
4.
5.

YOUR FAVORITES:

1. _____

2. _____

3. _____

4. _____

5. _____

2. IF YOU WERE STRANDED ON A DESERT ISLAND . . . Ask your new girlfriend what she would bring along. It's an interesting way to learn what's most important to her. Then you can share what you'd need to survive.

3. BEST DAY/WORST DAY OF YOUR LIFE. This one's a little more intense, so you should probably save it for a time when you feel you and your new girlfriend are really starting to get close. Begin with the best day. (Maybe it's the day your parents told you you were going to have a little brother. Or maybe it's when you performed the lead in the school play.) Give your bud the full details about what happened. Then ask for her best experience. After you've shared giggles and smiles over happy times, it's okay to get into the heavier stuff, if you want.

4. WHAT WOULD YOU DO IF . . . ? Hypothetical situations are always fun, and can reveal a lot about a person. Have your friend answer these questions:

? What would you do if your crush asked you out?

? What would you do if the world was going to blow up in twenty-four hours?

? What would you do if you were never allowed to drive?

? What would you do if you could switch places with anyone in the world?

? What would you do if you had the choice between spending the day with your favorite boy band or winning a million dollars?

See how easy that was? Once you get past the "What if nobody likes me?" fear, making friends is pretty simple—and fun.

So what happens when you find out your newest, best girl-friend is facing a truly tough time? You support her in any way you can. Read on to find out how.